"I have to leave here, Caitlyn. I have to leave here very soon."

When more of her hair slid free, she pulled off the hat and, with a nervous flutter, fanned her face with its broad brim. "I know you can't help me. But at least you don't treat me like some melodramatic little girl."

"First of all, you'd be crazy not to be upset after everything you've been through." Finally giving in to the need to touch her, he took her hand and stroked his thumb across her knuckles. "And believe me, I have never seen you as a little girl, not for a single moment."

Leaning closer, he skimmed his lips over her soft cheek and whispered into her ear, "It's a woman that I'm touching, a woman that I dream of. Or do you need a reminder of that, Caitlyn?"

COLLEEN THOMPSON

PHANTOM OF THE FRENCH QUARTER

Harlequin®

TORONTO NEW YORK LONDON
AMSTERDAM PARIS SYDNEY HAMBURG
STOCKHOLM ATHENS TOKYO MILAN MADRID
PRAGUE WARSAW BUDAPEST AUCKLAND

To every booklover who's ever passed along a favorite story and told a friend, a sister or a perfect stranger, "You absolutely *have* to read this."

Recycling programs
for this product may
not exist in your area.

ISBN-13: 978-0-373-74623-1

PHANTOM OF THE FRENCH QUARTER

Copyright © 2011 by Colleen Thompson

ABOUT THE AUTHOR

After beginning her career writing historical romance novels, Colleen Thompson turned to writing the contemporary romantic suspense she loves in 2004. Since then, her work has been honored with the Texas Gold Award, along with nominations for RITA®, Daphne du Maurier, and multiple reviewers' choice honors, along with starred reviews from *RT Book Reviews* and *Publishers Weekly*. A former teacher living with her family in the Houston area, Colleen has a passion for reading, hiking and dog rescue. Visit her online at www.colleen-thompson.com.

Books by Colleen Thompson

HARLEQUIN INTRIGUE
1286—CAPTURING THE COMMANDO
1302—PHANTOM OF THE FRENCH QUARTER

CAST OF CHARACTERS

Caitlyn Villaré—A beautiful young tour guide with a passion for old French Quarter cemeteries, Caitlyn will do whatever it takes to save her fledgling business—even if that means trusting the mesmerizing dark-eyed stranger she first glimpsed among the tombs.

Marcus Le Carpentier—Brooding and mysterious, this funerary art photographer has every reason to avoid police attention. Yet he cannot ignore the evidence his images have captured...or the smoldering attraction that threatens to ignite each time he encounters Caitlyn.

Josiah Paine—Caitlyn's hot-tempered former boss was furious that his best tour guide left to start a rival business. Has his thirst for vengeance gone beyond his angry words?

Max Lafitte—Jealous of Caitlyn's overnight success, does this aging tour guide have a far older reason to despise her?

Mrs. Eva Rill—Hidden beneath her black veil, this mysterious white-haired woman bristles with angry accusations—accusations that may only be a ruse to lure Caitlyn to her death.

Reuben Pierce—Hired to protect Caitlyn from the dangers of the Quarter, this retired cop-turned-bodyguard sees no greater threat than the fugitive photographer who seems so determined to spirit her away.

Chapter One

In an old French Quarter cemetery that cradled saints and sinners alike, dawn stained the slumbering fog bloodred. Layer after layer, it awakened, rising like the resurrected dead and swirling in soft eddies around the young woman cutting through it.

"It has to be here somewhere," Caitlyn Villaré called over her shoulder. Tension tightened her voice, and perspiration curled damp tendrils of long blond hair that clung to the fair skin at her temples and behind her neck. Her hand swished impatiently through the clotted June air, disturbing a small cloud of biting gnats.

From the next row of graves, a bull of a man wearing a rumpled chino blazer and a salt-and-pepper buzz cut shot her a grim look. "Let's not get your hopes up too high. I saw the rock that old bat was wearing, and if some lowlife caught sight of it out here..."

Reuben Pierce let the words die, but his grim

brown eyes did the talking for him. An old friend of her father's, the retired cop served as her assistant, fellow tour guide and bodyguard. Or *babysitter,* as Caitlyn thought when she was most exasperated with her overprotective older sister, Jacinth.

But he was right, Caitlyn admitted to herself. As soon as the two of them had escorted her party of tourists out through the cemetery gates last night, unsavory types had undoubtedly descended, trolling for any leavings—and hoping to surprise any straggler foolish enough to return for a private viewing.

Only last month, a lone tourist—not one of her clients, thank goodness—had been found here, his pockets turned out and his throat slashed, his cooling corpse lying in a congealing pool of blood. She shivered at the thought of it, hurrying her steps, and said to Reuben, "If I don't find that ring, that horrible old woman will tell everyone I stole it."

Caitlyn's stomach tightened with the memory of the shriveled crone, a tiny, wrinkled figure who'd worn a black lace veil over the silken white coil of her hair. At first Caitlyn had taken her attire for a costume, not unlike the gypsy storyteller outfits she herself wore to help enliven her tales of New Orleans's famous cities of the dead. But at four o'clock this morning, when the old woman calling herself Eva Rill had furiously rapped her cane against Caitlyn's front door, she was still dressed entirely in black, right down to the little round hat with the raven's feathers and the lacy cloud of netting.

Widow's weeds, her getup would have been called in an earlier century, but Caitlyn, who loved costuming as much as any of her fellow theater students, imagined them the garments of a dark witch...or an Old World sorceress.

"You should have heard the shrieking," Caitlyn went on. "She said she'll file a complaint with the police if I don't return the ring by noon today. Swore she'll have my license pulled and I'll lose everything I've worked for... everything Jacinth and I are turning ourselves inside out to try to—"

With the fog lifting, she saw the roll of Reuben's eyes and heard his scoffing laughter.

"Come on, kiddo. Calm down. First of all, what kind of idiot wears a rock the size of a pigeon's egg around the Quarter after dark? Even a tourist should know better. And who's gonna honestly believe you could somehow manage to slip that ring right off her bony finger without her noticing and screaming bloody murder?"

"Josiah Paine, that's who." Caitlyn grew morose, thinking of her former boss, the man who'd taken a chance on hiring her not long after she and her sister had come to New Orleans to settle their grandmother's estate. They hadn't planned on staying in the city their mother had refused to speak of, the city where their father had been murdered when Caitlyn was an infant. Nor had the sisters planned on falling in love with the crumbling Esplanade Avenue mansion they'd inherited, or the decaying, magnolia-scented tales of a place that all too quickly felt like home.

"Or at least he'll pretend he buys it," she grumbled, "so he can scare off every potential customer in earshot."

"Paine can be a pain, all right." Reuben gave a shrug. "But the more he trash-talks your business, the more free advertising the fool's giving you. I've told him as much myself."

"I'd rather find the ring than test your theory." Caitlyn poked among the weeds screening a stone obelisk, her mood darkening with the memory of the night her former boss had erupted, accusing her of holding back tip money, which he claimed as his due.

She'd grown used to his moods, his tendency toward pitting the employees against one another, even his shouting, but that night he had laid hands on her, slamming her so hard against a wall that she'd found bruises later. Embarrassed that she'd put up with his abuse for so long, she'd told no one, instead walking out and putting the whole sordid episode behind her.

And savoring the sweet revenge of seeing her dramatic delivery and winning people skills earn her the sort of word of mouth his cowed and miserable employees never could. Though she still couldn't afford an office of her own, she was booking more and more business using her home phone and computer.

Caitlyn moved along the row of tombs, weathered structures built in deference to the high water table's alarming tendency to float coffins to the surface. Some of the houselike vaults, mausoleums and monuments were more recent, clearly well tended, while others tilted, crumbling within the confines of fenced familial plots. Losing sight of Reuben, she followed the route she had taken last night, the pathway leading to the cemetery's oldest section.

So intent was she on her search that she never noticed how the chorus of morning birds fell silent. Nor did she pay any heed to the fiery disk of the sun climbing above the bruised horizon.

Half-hidden by another spray of weeds, she caught the bloody wink of a ruby flanked by a pair of teardrop diamonds. Her heart leaping with joy and relief, she opened her mouth to call to Reuben.

And that was when she noticed that the ring adorned a finger. A finger on a hand so pale, it might have been chiseled out of marble.

A hand connected to the outstretched arm of a young woman lying on her side behind a tombstone, her features set and rigid, her long blond hair fanned out…

And her green eyes looking like those that stared back at Caitlyn from her mirror every morning.

Except that these were glassy, hollow, as dead as the girl who lay there and said nothing, though her open mouth, obscenely rimmed in still-moist red lipstick, remained forever frozen in a hell-born silent scream.

MARCUS LE CARPENTIER HAD HER in his sights. So ethereal, so fragile, she looked as though she might crumble into dust with the weight of the slivered sunbeam that pierced the fog layers like the devil's darning needle.

Like the light, his caress came from a distance, focused by a lens that captured the rising bands of moisture, the single, slanting ray and the wings of the stone angel atop the mossy tomb. He blew back thick dark hair from darker eyes, his skin tightening with delicious anticipation.

When he saw this dawn angel, Isaiah would be so pleased, but it was nothing compared to the pleasure Marcus himself was deriving from this moment.

Moving the tip of one long finger atop the

shutter button, he held his breath and framed the ethereal light, the mist, the haunting artwork he had come so very far and through so very much to—

A gasp caught his attention a split second before something struck him from behind, hard enough to send both his four-thousand-dollar camera and its case flying. As he fell, Marcus instinctively grabbed for the one indispensable, irreplaceable item he had left to his name.

It hit the hard stone corner of a raised vault with a splintering noise before bouncing off and striking the bricked surface below.

"No!" he shouted, as he fell down on hands and knees.

Adrenaline pounding through him, he leapt panting to his feet, his fists already rising to ward off another attack.

The blonde who'd fallen into him scrambled out of reach, an instant before a piercing scream erupted from her rounded mouth, quickly drawing a brute with a graying buzz cut and blood in his eyes.

"What did you *do* to her?" The huge man stepped from the mist to move in on him, his own fists raised like a prizefighter's.

Marcus stood his ground, an eerie calm icing his voice. "To *her*? Let's talk about what *she* did to my camera, plowing into me like that."

Though he towered over Marcus's six feet, the man with the buzzed hair stopped short, studying his younger, lighter adversary. With the force of a stare that made most fights unnecessary, Marcus kept the human pit bull at bay.

Meanwhile, the young woman, no older than her early twenties, finally found her voice. "Not *him,* Reuben. It's the—she's *dead!*"

Both men followed her pointing finger toward a body. A body even paler than the terrified blonde who had destroyed his camera.

In every other respect, they looked virtually identical. Beautiful, with rivers of hair like summer moonlight and rounded eyes green as the bayou.

Except that one was still as stone, with her mouth agape and a lurid line of color bruising her alabaster neck.

"Holy hell." Reuben jerked a cell phone from his rumpled jacket. "Who is—she looks almost like—"

"Like *me,* I know." Terror pinched the living woman's voice.

Marcus knelt beside the crumpled female, his hand reaching to confirm what his eyes already knew. The skin of her wrist was cool and unyielding, as well as pulseless. Along the underside of her bare outstretched arm—her top was sleeveless, and ink-black to match her short skirt—

he focused on the line of livid purple, then the bruising on her neck. The splash of blood at the hollow of her throat seemed garish in contrast to her otherwise unblemished pallor.

But not nearly as horrifying as the way the eyes glittered when a ray of sunlight pierced the fog.

Rising with an oath, Marcus backed away, taking in the unnatural sheen of the blond filaments, the glassy stare that, he saw with a jolt, was *real* glass. Turning his head to take in the living woman, he realized that the dead one didn't look like her, not really....

Even though someone had apparently taken pains to make her seem that way.

Reuben began speaking into the phone, reporting their location and the discovery of a corpse, so Marcus directed his attention to the living woman.

"That's a wig she's wearing," he pointed out. "And those eyes. They aren't natural, either."

She edged close enough that he could hear the quick rhythm of her breathing, could feel the nervous energy pulsing from her. Peering at the body, she said, "Why would someone *do* this?"

Don't get involved, warned the instinct that four years of running had honed to a keen edge. Yet the fear in her red-rimmed eyes, the popped pearl button on her ivory blouse and the torn knee of the pants that skimmed her slender body made her need so real and immediate, so *human,* that he couldn't stop himself from asking, "Who knew you would be here? Some admirer you've turned away? An ex-boyfriend who can't let go?"

Fear flashed over her beautiful features, and she shook her head. "There's no one like that, no one in a long time. But there was this old woman—she accused me of..."

Her trembling hand pointed to the ring the corpse was wearing, a ring with a stone so large, he suspected it was as artificial as the long blond hair and green eyes.

Why couldn't the body be a fake, too? A mannequin, arranged and decorated as a bad joke? But the cool flesh had felt all too human, and the horror of the gaping mouth was all too real.

Reuben flipped his phone shut and in a take-charge voice said, "Police are on their way. They'll want to talk to us."

Something in Marcus froze at those words. To hide his reaction, he turned away and scooped up his rattling Nikon, along with several small items that had fallen from the camera bag.

"Sorry I ran into you. It was just so—so awful, seeing her, that I—" the woman said before Reuben overrode her, his flat brown stare boring into Marcus.

"What're you doing out here at this hour?" The

huge man sounded coplike himself, suspicion tightening his clean-shaven jaw.

Marcus raised the camera in answer, then tossed back the question. "And the two of you were out here because…?"

"We were looking for a lost—" the woman started.

"That's none of his business, Caitlyn," Reuben warned her before his voice softened. "You're hurt."

"No, I'm fine. I'm…" She glanced down at a few drops of blood that had seeped through the torn material at her knee. Shaking her head, she said, "Never mind that."

She looked into Marcus's face, her expression a brand of innocence he'd forgotten existed in the world. "I'm Caitlyn Villaré, from Villar-A1 Tours. This is my assistant, Reuben Pierce."

Considering the difference in their ages and the man's obvious protectiveness, Marcus would have been less surprised to learn that Reuben was a doting father or an uncle. But not a sugar daddy, not to this angelic-looking blonde.

"We were looking for something one of my clients lost here last night," she told him. "A ring."

"I'm Ethan. Ethan Thornton." The lie came smoothly, honed by years of practice at using different names in different cities. Only this time, for the first time in memory, he felt the kick of conscience. "I have an interest in funerary art."

"You have an interest in taking pictures of dead girls, too?" Reuben challenged. "Maybe setting up your own—"

As Marcus fixed him with another cold stare, Caitlyn cut him off. *"Reuben,* this is horrible enough without you pointing fingers. I'm sorry, Mr. Thornton."

Reuben's expression said *he* wasn't, that he remained suspicious. But at least he backed off, muttering only a face-saving "Cops'll be here any minute. Guess we'll leave the questions to them."

The three of them stood in awkward silence, avoiding eye contact as they waited for—and, in Marcus's case, dreaded—the first sirens to pierce the delicate veil of birdsong.

Caitlyn glanced down at the body, then looked away quickly and hugged herself as a chill rippled over her flesh. "I've never seen someone—I mean, I was with my mother when she died of cancer. But that was nothing like this."

Reuben took her arm and steered her toward a stone bench. "Here, why don't you sit down? You've had a shock, and you're still bleeding. And there's no need to stand there looking at... it."

"Her," Caitlyn corrected, ignoring the damp

slab of concrete he was indicating. "She's still a person, isn't she? We can give her that much, at least."

Still a person. Soft and serious, her words slipped beneath Marcus's armor, beneath the skin itself. And he couldn't help but wonder, could a woman who found humanity in a grotesquely altered dead girl see a man like him, a man who'd fallen so far and so hard, as—

Too dangerous to go there, to allow himself to feel. At the moment, *thinking* was required. Thinking and watching until he finally found the right moment to fade into the background, to move on to the next city and forget those glassy, green eyes…along with their living mirror image in the face of Caitlyn Villaré.

Chapter Two

"Tell me more about the man who fled the scene before the officers arrived, the one who told you his name was Ethan Thornton." In the airless interview room at the police station, Detective Lorna Robinson leaned her considerable weight onto her forearms, flattening her flesh against the table. With her cropped, red-streaked hair and her chunky wooden jewelry, she locked in on Caitlyn with a striking hazel gaze a few shades lighter than her rich brown skin. "Could you describe him for me again?"

"Tall and on the slim side. His eyes were almost black." Caitlyn closed her own eyes in an attempt to find the words to describe him. Exhausted as she was from her interrupted sleep and the backwash of emotion, she wanted nothing more than to finish this discussion and go home. "His hair was wavy, long and dark brown."

"How long, would you say?"

"It brushed his shoulders, I think. A little

tousled but clean." There was so much more Caitlyn couldn't find the words for. How his hands were long and elegant as a sculptor's. How his gaze shifted, stone to liquid, with currents of thought running deep and swift beneath the espresso-colored surface.

How the sight of him, the rich timbre of his voice and the way he carried himself had sent attraction knifing through her. But she said nothing, knowing the tidal pull could only be an illusion, that shock had been what left her quaking—the discovery of a body that looked more like a sister to her than dark-haired Jacinth ever had.

A need to call Jacinth had Caitlyn's stomach clenching. But if she did, her older sister would rush home from the summer seminar she'd just begun teaching in Mississippi—and they desperately needed her earnings to pay the looming tax bill on the house.

Besides, Caitlyn was tired of being protected. Even more than that, she was sick of being treated like brilliant brunette Jacinth's idiot blonde sister, despite the fact that she'd graduated with high honors from a well-respected theater program last year, and had gotten a successful business up and running, mostly on her own, within months of her arrival in this city.

"Still with me, Ms. Villaré?" Straightening,

Detective Robinson tapped a pen against her notepad. "I asked, how was this Mr. Thornton dressed?"

Caitlyn frowned, considering. "His jeans were pretty faded. The shirt was loose, long sleeved, open at the throat. It was white, and kind of old-fashioned. *He* looked old-fashioned, too."

The detective looked up from her scribbling. "I thought you said he was young."

Caitlyn shook her head. "He *was* young, no more than his late twenties. It was just—the hair, the shirt. He might have stepped out of the Renaissance, or a pirate movie."

Detective Robinson smiled. "You have a very different way of describing people, know that?"

Caitlyn shrugged. "Even storytelling has its occupational hazards. So what did Reuben tell your partner about Mr. Thornton?"

When he'd been ushered toward a different interview room, Caitlyn had protested, but Reuben had shushed her. The retired cop had told her in his brusque voice, *Don't worry,* chère. *It's just procedure. And it's not like either of us has anything to hide.*

"Right now, I'm only interested in what *you* think." Annoyance furrowed Detective Robinson's brow. "You're sure you didn't see him leave? Or hear a vehicle or something?"

"At first I thought he'd gone off with one of the officers or something."

"We'll work on tracking him down. Would've made it a lot easier if he'd shown up in the system under the name he gave you."

"You mean he *lied?*" She knew it was ridiculous, but Caitlyn took the deception personally. The stranger had looked straight at her, with those ink-dark eyes, and he'd lied to her point-blank.

A spark of humor lit the detective's eyes. "You really *are* young, aren't you, hon?"

Caitlyn barely had time to feel insulted before Robinson added, "I can tell you from experience, there're plenty of citizens out there who aren't too eager to get involved in police matters. For a whole variety of reasons."

Caitlyn felt the blood drain from her face. "Of course, I understand that, but he—you don't think he could have been the one who...?" She pictured the still-unidentified woman's marble-pale skin, the gaping, bloodless mouth set in a voiceless scream. Had the man Caitlyn had literally run into after the discovery, the man who'd looked as stunned as she felt, really been a killer?

Was it possible anyone so handsome could do such ugly, sick things? Shivering, she hugged her arms, though the room was warm and stuffy.

"Too soon to say." Pulling a card from the pocket of her dark brown jacket, Detective Robinson added, "But you hear from him or see him, call me—any time. It's possible this man could pose a danger."

An unspoken truth hung like smoke between them, and Caitlyn saw the reminder in the detective's eyes of how closely she resembled the dead woman. Or how likely it seemed that the corpse had been deliberately altered to look like her.

Though Caitlyn still held out a thimble's worth of hope, no one had suggested the resemblance was coincidental, especially after she'd described Eva Rill's threats at her home last night—the same threats that had led Caitlyn to the body.

"Don't worry. I'll definitely call," said Caitlyn, relieved to think the interview had finally come to an end.

But the detective wasn't finished. "Let's get back to the old woman," she said. "This Mrs. Rill, was she acting strange on your tour last night?"

Caitlyn sighed. "I thought the black veil and the dress seemed odd. But we saw weirder last night—everything from piercings and a rainbow Mohawk to a bunch of handsy frat boys with more hurricanes than sense inside them," she said, referring to a drink popular with Bourbon Street revelers. "So, no, I didn't notice one quiet little old lady in particular."

"Until she showed up at four in the morning to accuse you of theft."

When Caitlyn nodded, the detective wondered aloud, "How would she know where you lived in the first place?"

"Why don't you ask her? I gave you her number at least an hour ago."

Last night the old woman had insisted she take it down so Caitlyn could call her if she "decided to return" the missing ring.

"I went ahead and tried it after I showed you in here. The number's to a mortuary over in the Garden District. They never heard of any Eva Rill."

The female detective leaned in even closer, piercing Caitlyn with a needle-sharp gaze. "How 'bout you?"

Shocked by the woman's sudden change in tone, Caitlyn snapped, "*Me?* Are you—are you insinuating that I know Mrs. Rill, or made up the story about her coming to threaten me last night? Why? Why would you think such a—"

Sound echoed through the small room as Detective Robinson tore a sheet of paper off her pad and then ripped it several times. "Let me show you why, Ms. Villaré," she said as she printed large block letters, one to a scrap.

She turned the letters around, allowing Caitlyn to read: *E-V-A R-I-L-L.*

Leaning in, the detective asked her, "You're

absolutely certain you don't have anything you want to tell me?"

"Like what?" Caitlyn shot back as she watched the dark hands rearranging letters, sliding them around like the pieces in a shell game.

Sliding them around until they spelled her own name: V-I-L-L-A-R-E.

AN OLDER SILVER CHEVY RUMBLED like low thunder beside the wrought-iron fence that hemmed in a Grand Lady. Or at least that was what his mother would have called the towering white plantation-style mansion, with its Greek Revival columns and elegant two-story veranda.

Beside the house stood a venerable live oak, its twisted Spanish moss-cloaked branches reminding Marcus of an old man scowling at the threadbare fugitive parked near his front door.

"Just keep driving," Marcus told himself. But his gaze remained fixed on the Villaré house, a place that whispered his name more loudly than anywhere he'd wandered.

But then, New Orleans's siren song had been calling from the first moments he had smelled the Mississippi River's muddy perfume, heard the raucous strains of Preservation Hall jazz, and tasted the café au lait and beignets he'd sampled near Jackson Square. By the time he'd made it to the cemetery yesterday, what was meant to be a brief visit for a few shots had taken on the weight and texture of homecoming.

As well it might, for the New Orleans he'd left at the age of five was the last place he had felt safe. The last place his mother's arms had ever held him.

Now it was the last place, the riskiest place, he could possibly be. And the Villaré mansion was by far the most dangerous spot in it.

Forget it. Forget her, breathed a voice he recognized as reason's.

Yet after one last look around, Marcus climbed out of the car he'd chosen for its anonymity, a Chevy whose plates were regularly, if not quite legally, traded.

Beneath a steel-gray sky he approached the front gate, his palms sweating in the sultry afternoon heat. The tips of his fingers made damp impressions on the manila envelope containing the print. Not the photograph he'd gone to the cemetery specifically to capture, but an inadvertent image he couldn't talk himself into ignoring any more than he could forget the two blondes, one living and one dead, he had seen this morning.

You still have time to turn around.

Iron hinges creaked and he was inside, telling himself he could be safe and away in seconds as he walked up the steps and knelt beside the oversized front door. Before he could slide the envelope beneath the mat and leave, the door cracked open as far as the chain latch would allow.

"Reuben's calling the police now."

His gaze snapped to Caitlyn Villaré's face, peering from behind the door.

Rising slowly so he wouldn't scare her, he offered her the envelope. "Camera's broken, but there were shots still on the memory card," he told her. "Including one I thought you might find interesting."

Rather than reaching for the envelope, she scowled at him. "Why did you leave earlier? Why did you run from the police?"

He tried a smile. "Didn't run. I just left. Who has time to waste getting tangled up with—"

"I don't like being lied to, *Ethan.*" Her gaze intensified, breaching levies he had spent years building.

"All right, then." He drew a deep breath and said, "I'm Marcus," without understanding why. He hadn't revealed his name in years now. Hadn't thought he ever would again.

"How did you find me…Marcus?" she asked.

If speaking his real name after so long was a relief, hearing it on her lips brought such a rush of pleasure that he couldn't speak until she began to close the door, apparently giving up on an answer.

"Your website had a number," he explained,

wondering what had happened again. "It was easy doing a reverse search on the net to find the address."

"Of course," Caitlyn murmured. "I guess that you and the old lady must have had the same idea. Jacinth really was right about not using our home number for the business."

"She was right. It's not safe."

Caitlyn rolled her eyes. "Thank you, Captain Obvious."

He snorted and then glanced over his shoulder. "Take the photo. Give it to the cops when they show up."

"Why?" she asked. "What's in the picture?"

He shook his head, while behind him, thunder murmured, an uneasy harbinger of predicted storms. "Nothing, maybe. Could be just another cemetery visitor. A widow, out to see her—"

"Let me have that." The door strained against the taut chain, and Caitlyn's hand shot out, pale and delicate.

Marcus knew he should shove the envelope at her and take off. But if her pit bull of an assistant really was here, wouldn't he be pushing forward to deal with Marcus himself by now? Innocent as she seemed, Marcus suspected the sweet-faced blonde had lied to him about Reuben's presence. Maybe she had lied about the police being on the way, too.

Looking into her vulnerable green eyes, he thought of lingering to find out if he was right. Then he reminded himself that his future and his freedom weren't his alone to gamble.

But his instinct to protect wasn't listening to reason, so he slid the eight-by-ten out of the envelope and pointed to a figure he hadn't noticed out in the cemetery that morning. Using his laptop and a portable photo printer, he'd enlarged a detail near the margin: a tiny, shriveled woman peering from behind a houselike tomb. Silhouetted by the shadowed dawn, she'd been caught in the act of lifting a black veil from her face, a movement that revealed the furtive malevolence of her expression.

"I have to leave," he said to Caitlyn, "but I thought you should have this. It may be nothing, but—"

"Wait, Marcus. Let me look at that." Unlatching the door, she snatched the print from his hand and studied it intently, noticing that a smoke-gray Persian cat had emerged and was winding around her ankles. "This is my customer, from last night's tour. The one who lost her ring."

"The ring the dead woman was wearing?" he asked, putting together the pieces.

Caitlyn gave him an appraising look before nodding at the photo. "She stood right here on this doorstep at four this morning. Shrieking like a banshee that I stole the thing."

Marcus glanced over his shoulder before saying, "To lure you to that cemetery. To that body."

As the cat stared at him disdainfully, Caitlyn nodded. "I can't think of any other reason. Did you see anyone else this morning? Any other people nearby?"

He opened his mouth to speak, then snapped it closed again to listen to the thinnest thread of sound. A sound that gradually grew louder, beneath the lightest pattering of the raindrops that had just begun to fall.

A siren, he realized as he backed away, head shaking. Obviously someone really had called the police after all.

"Wait!" she called. "Don't leave. I didn't…"

But the spell had finally shattered. Remembering his obligations at last, Marcus had turned away already. He broke into a loping run, vaulting the low gate to save the second it would have taken to pull it open.

As he swung into the gray sedan, he jammed the key into the ignition, then drove off wondering if Caitlyn had been stalling him from the start. Intentionally delaying his departure until the police arrived to take him into custody.

Chapter Three

His grandmother had collected doll babies by the hundreds, which his mother had arranged on shelves around the room where he'd slept as a boy.

How he'd hated those damned dolls, staring at him through the days and nights. How he'd pleaded with his mother to box them up, to let him put up his sports pennants and his model racecars—the kinds of decorations he wouldn't have to hide from other guys.

Year after year she had stubbornly refused, saying it would be disrespectful of Grandmama's memory to hide them all away, and that the narrow bungalow—a damned shack, really—was far too small to put them elsewhere.

"Then keep them in your room," he had at first demanded and then pleaded, tears streaking down his red face.

But they both knew she wouldn't, that the men

who visited her at night could never do their dirty business with all those glass eyes staring at them.

And after a while, it was all right. He grew used to his silent companions. Grew to prefer them to the classmates he couldn't invite over anyway.

DRIPPING FROM THE RAIN, Reuben returned from the hardware store, and Caitlyn quickly filled him in about her visitor.

"You opened the door to that man? Spoke to him like some old friend?" Shaking his head, he set the rain-spattered bag with the new deadbolts he'd gone to buy, after insisting the house needed to be better secured, on the kitchen counter.

Like nearly every part of their white elephant of a legacy, the once-rich wood needed attention. But that she could ignore for now, unlike the faltering air conditioner that had left the whole house stewing in its juices.

Back in Ohio, where she'd grown up, a summer rain would have cooled things. Here, it only made June's heat more oppressive.

"I kept the chain latched," she explained. "And I thought if we talked, I could find out—"

"Fat lot of good that would've done you if he'd had a gun. This is a serious situation. You've gotta use your head."

She looked away, feeling her jaw tighten, wanting to explain that she had. She'd learned to trust her instincts about people, even if she couldn't explain them in any way that made sense to Reuben and her sister, who thought the world was built of hard facts and right angles. And who assumed that anyone who saw it otherwise was hopelessly naive.

"Off the counter, Sin," she scolded her grandmother's ancient Persian.

Fluffy the cat, whom the sisters had rechristened "Sinister" in honor of his hateful, orange-eyed stare, hissed at her before twitching his tail and jumping down to pointedly ignore her.

"It's my job to keep you safe." Reuben's tone softened a fraction. "So let's not get all girlie on me."

"He told me his name's really Marcus." She felt an echo of the electrical zing of intuition assuring her that this time he had told the truth. That he wouldn't hurt her. "Would he have done that if I'd hidden and speed-dialed the police?"

"Marcus *who?* He show you any ID to back up that claim?"

"Oh, sure. And volunteered a cheek swab so you could run his DNA, too."

Reuben gave a snort and grinned before changing the subject. "Anyway, what's this about some picture?"

Still annoyed, she laid it on the counter. "It's

Mrs. Rill," she said, for lack of another name to call the woman.

She had already filled him in on Lorna Robinson's disturbingly clever anagram trick, the way the detective had hinted that Caitlyn's involvement might be more than that of a potential victim. That perhaps *someone* might have cooked up a sick way to gain publicity for her fledgling tour-guide business.

Reuben had laughed when Caitlyn told him, and promised to call an old friend from his years on the force—Detective Robinson's partner, Davis— to set the cops straight about that ridiculous idea.

Sweaty and exhausted, Caitlyn wasn't sure which she found more upsetting: to be suspected of a crime or laughed off as a suspect.

Though he hadn't touched the photo, Reuben studied it intently. "That's the old bat, all right. I wonder how she's mixed up in this? Can't see a frail old biddy like her as the killer."

At the word "killer," the dead woman's face flashed through Caitlyn's mind. Only this time, she thought about the green eyes. Glass eyes, the same as she'd seen...

"Josiah Paine's a hunter," she blurted. "He has heads hanging all over his office."

"Former employees?" Reuben asked drily.

"Deer, mostly, and this poor, moth-eaten

black bear. An armadillo, too, and there's even a whole stuffed alligator." She shuddered, recalling how creeped out she'd been by his "curiosities," though he swore the customers loved them. "Those animals all have glass eyes, too."

"So you're thinking…?" Reuben sketched out an arch with the tip of his finger, a bridge from one idea to the next. "That's a pretty big stretch, from Bambi hunter to psycho killer. What sportsman doesn't have a few old trophies hangin' 'round his—"

"We already know he can't stand me."

"And I can't stand Creole cookin'. Doesn't mean I'm gonna kill and stuff a Cajun chef to intimidate them others." He shook his head. "Listen, sugar, you're one heck of a tour guide— I never get tired of hearin' you tell stories 'bout the ghosts of old N'awlins. But you'd better leave the cookin' to the Cajuns and the detectin' to the pros."

Heat stung her cheeks. "Don't patronize me, Reuben. I'm serious about him."

"Then tell it to the police—" he gestured toward the photo but still avoided touching it "—when we turn this thing over to 'em."

When Detectives Robinson and Davis arrived to collect the photo, Caitlyn brought up Josiah Paine immediately, but Robinson's partner, a pudgy, balding man with woolly gray brows and small, pointed teeth, was quick to shrug it off. "I know Josiah real well. Sure, he burns a little hot, likes to shoot his mouth off, but under all that, he's a teddy bear. A guy you can always count on for a nice donation when we're raising money for a cop's sick kid or something."

Looking toward Reuben, Davis added, "You remember him, don't ya, Rube? Picks up rounds at Tujague's every now and then."

"That's what I was tellin' Caitlyn," Reuben answered. "Paine's a lot of things, but he's no killer."

Caitlyn might have grown up in Ohio, but she recognized Good Old Boydom when she heard it. Frustrated, she tried zeroing in on Robinson. "You only *think* you know him."

Detective Robinson merely frowned and changed the subject. "Didn't you call us about some picture?"

"In here," Reuben said, and four sets of footsteps echoed on the marble tile leading beneath an immense chandelier hanging high above them from a vaulted ceiling embellished with hand-painted nymphs and satyrs. The nineteenth-century fresco had cracked and peeled in places, as badly in need of restoration as the rest of this white elephant of a legacy. But that didn't stop Caitlyn from loving it completely—and hoping, scheming and praying for some way she and her sister might hold on to it.

They passed the formal parlor, filled with prissy, somewhat dusty furnishings that looked far too fine to sit on, and Detective Davis whistled through his small teeth. "Nice place."

Caitlyn thanked him and said, "The photo's right here, in the kitchen."

After giving them a chance to look it over, she said, "She's definitely the woman from last night's tour. 'Eva Rill.'"

Her fingertips formed quotes around the name.

Detective Davis produced an evidence bag and slipped the photo inside. "Maybe we can circulate this, find someone who knows her. If we can bring her in for questioning, check out her family and associates, it's a good bet she'll lead us to the killer. Best bet we have," he said, and turned to Reuben, "unless we can track down this Marcus fellow you told me about when you called."

"I don't think he's involved," Caitlyn said. "I got the feeling he's just a really private person. That's why he didn't want to be drawn into—"

"We have to consider the possibility," Detective Robinson said, her light hazel eyes serious, "that Mrs. Rill is this guy's accomplice—maybe his own grandma, for all we know. Because whoever committed this crime may very well be a man obsessed with you. Sexually obsessed."

"Why would you say…" Caitlyn was no prude, but she found it hard to get the word out past the sudden lump in her throat. "Why would you say *sexually?* How can you be certain the killer's even a man?" *Let alone* that *man?* she added silently. And what kind of woman would help her grandson murder someone, anyway?

The two detectives shared an uncomfortable glance.

"What?" Caitlyn pressed. "Someone sent me to find that body, someone who made that poor girl look as much like me as he could. So I have the right to know what this is about."

"I'm afraid that the dead girl, a Megan Lansky," Detective Robinson said soberly, "appears to have been sexually assaulted."

"Wait a minute. I know that name," Reuben said. "She's that missing girl—I saw her parents on the five o'clock news, pleadin' to find out if anybody's seen her. Pretty little thing."

Detective Davis nodded gravely, then turned to Caitlyn. "Lansky was a Tulane student, disappeared a couple of nights ago after partying on Bourbon Street. Her friends told Missing Persons she'd mentioned hooking up with some group going on a cemetery tour."

A chill slithered along Caitlyn's backbone, then coiled in her stomach. "Are you sure she's the girl we found this morning?"

"Poor kid's father just ID'd her."

Caitlyn's knees loosened, and she braced herself against the counter. "Do you—do you have a picture of her? The way she looked...*before?*"

Detective Davis quickly produced one. In it, Megan Lansky smiled, a beautiful girl with wavy, light brown hair and sparkling blue eyes. Beautiful and so young, someone who should be near the beginning of life's journey instead of lying, pale and bloodless, in a cold drawer at the morgue.

Was she dead because some sick person had thought she resembled Caitlyn? Could it have been some crazy customer from one of Caitlyn's tours? She thought of drunken troublemakers and one lovesick young man who had sent her a half-dozen admiring emails and phoned repeatedly, coming on way too strong in his quest for a date. But none of them seemed dangerous—or at least not the brand of dangerous that led to things like rape and murder. To gouging out blue eyes and replacing them with green glass.

Tears leaking, Caitlyn shook her head. Her voice trembled, but somehow she managed to remain coherent. "I don't think I've ever seen her. What about you, Reuben? Could she have come on one of our tours this week?"

Reuben studied the photo for some time before he shook his head. "Damned shame, a young girl like that. Makes me want to kick the guts out of the sick bastard who would…"

He closed his eyes, his face reddening. "Twenty-eight years on the force, you'd've thought I'd grown myself a tougher shell. Maybe it's for the best I went and got myself…"

Davis's woolly eyebrows drew closer together. "So neither one of you knew Megan?"

To be absolutely certain, Caitlyn checked their receipts, but Megan Lansky wasn't listed among the credit card payments.

"You might try the other tour services," she suggested, and couldn't resist adding for good measure, "You might try Josiah Paine."

HOURS LATER, SHE WAS STILL UPSET as Reuben drove her toward the cemetery in his Crown Victoria, a great boat of a car he said reminded him of his days driving police cruisers. Considering the threatening thunder and a new round of storms forecast for this evening, she thought a real boat might come in handy before this night was over.

Hunched over the wheel, he shot a scowl in her direction. "You should be back at home, *chère,* doors and windows locked tight, and me bunking on one of them fancy horsehair excuses for a sofa."

Caitlyn smoothed her skirt, a gauzy, handkerchief-hemmed creation she had made from the evening gowns of a grandmother she had barely known. "Unless you want your paycheck bouncing, we need to get out there and work."

The black car jerked to a stop as a light went from yellow to red. "You think I give a damn about money right now? With some sick—" Cutting himself off, he shook his head. "This is way bigger than money. This is your life we're talkin' 'bout here."

"That's right," she said, heart thumping. "It's *my* life. And I still mean to live it."

And that meant she needed to get back to work to pay the bills. More than that, she needed to feel the words that flowed with every story, to watch the rapt eyes of her listeners and hear collective gasps. Her drama professors and scouts alike had assured her she had ample talent, presence and beauty to command the stage or screen. But in one audition after the next, she had lacked some crucial, unteachable ingredient: a real connection with the audience. She'd finally discovered such a bond while sharing the stories she'd collected volunteering in the old French Quarter nursing home where her grandmother spent her last days, a place Caitlyn had gone in the hope of learning something of the woman she and Jacinth had never been allowed to know.

A die-hard history major, Jacinth brushed off the tales Caitlyn collected as "unsubstantiated melodrama," but even she had been unable to hide her excitement over one involving their own ancestor, Victoria Villaré, who had allegedly used a secret passage to spy on Union officers who had occupied her home during the Civil War. For long months after hearing of it, the sisters had searched in vain for some sign of a hidden doorway, but for Caitlyn, the proof had never been the point.

A block from the cemetery, they found a parking space. As they climbed out, thunder rumbled, and Reuben asked, "You sure about this? It's gonna be a night fit for one of them ole *rougaroux* you like to scare the tourists with."

When an image of Megan Lansky's bone-white corpse flashed through Caitlyn's mind, she shivered at the thought of the legendary Cajun werewolf, a zombielike monster said to drain its victims dry. Though the French called them *loup-garou,* the Cajun version was every bit as frightening.

But *rougaroux* weren't stranglers, nor were they controlled by tiny old ladies who used creepy anagrams as names and claimed mortuary numbers as their home phone.

Reaching onto the backseat floorboard, Caitlyn grabbed a pair of umbrellas, along with her flashlight, and forced herself to grin at Reuben. "You know as well as I do," she said, her voice only a bit shaky, "these 'dark and stormy nights' are great for business—and if I don't get back on the horse tonight, I'm afraid I'll never set foot in this cemetery again."

Twenty minutes later, she was sharing her great, great, great grandmother's story with the dozen or so tourists who joined her not fifty yards from the spot where she had found the body. Senior citizens, urban hipsters and lovers of the paranormal, she held them all spellbound as they stood beside the wall vault containing the remains of more than a dozen Villarés, including the famous Victoria, Caitlyn's grandmother Marie... everyone except her father, whose body had never been recovered from the swamp, where he'd been murdered by a fishing buddy.

As thunder rumbled all around them and the low clouds' bellies flickered with lightning, only Reuben Pierce seemed immune to the mood she was creating. He constantly wandered the group's perimeter, aiming his flashlight between rows of tombs, and bristled when another tour group encroached on their territory.

Edging closer to where he stood while her clients took pictures of the surrounding tombs, she whispered as the wind gasped through the nearby treetops, "Relax, it's only Mumbling Max. You know how he's been lately."

"Mumbling Max" Lafitte was the guide who'd

taught her the ropes for Paine, a balding, gray-haired man whose uninspired performances quickly convinced her that she could do a whole lot better. Dull as he was, Max had hated being outshone by a young upstart—and hated it even more when his boss repeatedly humiliated him about it. To get even with her, Max was always horning in on her tours, trying to drown out her stories with his drone.

A cool breeze stirred her hair, a welcome breath of fresh air that was quickly followed by the rain.

"Last week's offer stands," Reuben said above the patter on the tops of their umbrellas. "You say the word, I'll have that weasel scamperin' outta here like—"

He never had the chance to finish, as a deafening explosion and a blinding white streak filled the air. With a reflexive shriek echoed by the scattering tourists, Caitlyn dropped the flashlight and her umbrella, and ran, instinctively avoiding the sharp crack of falling wood from the lightning-struck tree.

But she only made it a few steps before something struck her. With a pain like a hatchet splitting her skull, the chaotic scene fell silent and all the world winked out.

Chapter Four

Before Marcus's stunned eyes, the night shattered into stark frames. Blackness and confusion. Lightning flash-lit still shots.

A dark figure dragging off a fallen blonde. Dragging her away to—

No! Shaking off the shock of the ear-splitting boom, Marcus didn't think but reacted solely on instinct. An instinct to protect Caitlyn Villaré at all costs.

Hurtling through the pitch dark, he struck like a guided missile. The force of his leap knocked the kidnapper off his feet.

Knocked him down and made him drop her as the rain crashed down in blinding sheets. Marcus ducked two broad swings before coming up with a spinning hook kick that should have taken his opponent's head off.

Instead, he heard a startled grunt and felt the impact as his foot struck either the man's shoulder or his chest. Rather than staying to throw more punches, Marcus's opponent turned and vanished, out of sight and out of reach.

But had he left for good? Or was he only waiting for a second opportunity?

And how could Marcus follow and catch him, when he couldn't possibly leave Caitlyn lying, crumpled and unconscious, in the rain?

As HE PACED the cramped motel room hours later, Marcus's pulse throbbed at his temples and his heartbeat boomed in his ears. What the hell had he done? Had his lonely, nomadic existence worn him down so badly that he'd decided to crush it out like a burned-down cigarette?

If I wasn't a criminal before, I am now, he realized, as he stared at the beautiful blonde woman sleeping in his bed. Still, for all his remorse, his fingers itched to touch the shutter button, to record the contrast of the angel in repose against the grungy hell of this bottom-rung dive.

Great idea—give them proof you're an obsessed animal.

Regardless of the temptation, he knew it would be days before the lens arrived to fix his camera, and probably only hours before he was taken into custody for kidnapping.

How would he explain the drastic steps he'd taken to safeguard Caitlyn Villaré—or the unanswerable yearning that her presence, the very thought of her, set off in his soul?

Insane. You've had some kind of break with reality. Wasn't that what the shrinks would say when he tried to make them understand? The cops and the DA would have another name for it, especially once they discovered the charges against him back in Pennsylvania.

Murder, arson—each flare of memory seared his awareness, choked him with the bitter ash of regret.

But he had to keep his mind on present problems, such as the item he had accidentally scooped up in the cemetery while collecting the things that had spilled from his camera case. The new evidence that had driven him to risk contacting Caitlyn again.

He thought, too, of the low-life motel clerk, the one witness who had seen him walking in supporting Caitlyn.

"Your girl have one too many?" The skinny kid had laughed, his beaky nose poking through a screen of greasy hair and his vintage heavy-metal T-shirt as holey as his black jeans.

"Just tired," Marcus had assured him.

The clerk's leer said that he knew better, and he'd handed Marcus a card with his name, Craven, and a number scribbled on it. "You decide you need somebody to drop her somewhere later, just text me your room number. For a little cash, I'm your man to make things happen. Anything you want."

Marcus had passed Bird Beak two twenties to ensure that he wouldn't be disturbed, but he had to take it on faith that Craven was exactly what he appeared to be: an opportunistic lowlife who would sooner sell his grandma than talk to the police.

As light rain pattered against a grimy window, Caitlyn moaned and shifted. Marcus's relief slid free in a sigh, because if he'd been wrong and she failed to regain consciousness, if she—he scarcely dared to think it—died, all of this would be for nothing, and he might as well go turn himself in.

At the chipped sink, he ran warm water over a thin washcloth, then wrung it out, and returned to sit beside the bed and gently clean her face. She stirred, and he smiled, the first real smile that had crossed his features in… He shook his head, unable, or perhaps unwilling, to remember a time when he'd still been his own man, pursuing fame instead of hiding from it.

"Caitlyn," he said softly. "Caitlyn, can you hear me?"

Her eyelids cracked open, lamplight reflecting off irises the shade of moss touched by the morning sunlight. Relief washed over him, a floodtide of emotion.

She stared at him for a moment before those eyes flashed open and she scrambled away until her back was pressed against the peeling, laminated headboard. Looking around wildly, she cried, "What—where am I? What are you doing here? What happened?"

But she didn't scream—not yet—something Marcus counted as a blessing.

"Let me explain," he said, rushing to cram in as much as he could before the inevitable explosion. "You've had an accident, or not really an accident. I'm pretty sure someone hit you on the head. I caught him dragging you off in the chaos after the lightning strike."

He could still smell the ozone, still hear the tourists screaming and scattering as a male voice—Reuben's?—warned them to stay together for their safety. But Marcus's eyes, already adjusted to the darkness from his long wait, had seen more than the others—perhaps because Caitlyn had been his sole focus from the spot where he had watched in silence, mentally framing every angle for a photo he had no camera to take. And waiting for his chance to…

"I had to get you out of there," he tried to explain.

She shuddered, revulsion twisting her mouth. "So you could abduct me, drag me to some sleazy hotel and—"

"No! It wasn't like that. I never touched you that way. I only meant to keep you safe."

She tugged at her peasant blouse, which had fallen off her shoulder, and narrowed her eyes. "Then why not take me to a hospital? I was—"

Her hand drifted toward the side of her head, and before he could warn her, she was hissing in pain, fingers coming away tacky with coagulating blood.

"Ow…" Her face lost color, putting him in mind of the dead girl's from that morning. "He— whoever hit me could've killed me."

"You've been stirring, making noises. I didn't think you were under too deep," Marcus said, but even to his ears, the excuse rang hollow. "And once I'd taken you—because I was afraid he'd come after you again—there was no way I could go anywhere the police could…where they could get hold of me."

"So instead you disappeared again, like some sort of phantom—only this time, you've dragged me with you." Her expression hardening, she said flatly, "You're on the run from the law, aren't you? That's why you wouldn't get involved this morning. Why you were afraid to stick around tonight."

Her eyes flicked toward the softly shifting light of a slow-motion slideshow on his laptop. His photos from the cemeteries, running as a screen saver. But she said nothing of them.

"I was afraid for *you* this evening," he insisted. "You have no idea how damned hard I've prayed—"

"To what gods, Marcus?" The stone angel's image, miraculously captured in the instant before she'd knocked the camera from his hands that morning, flashed across the screen. "Do they have a separate pantheon for stalkers?"

"This is the thanks I get for saving you? For watching your every breath these past two hours? I'm no damned stalker, Caitlyn. I swear to you, I'm only—"

She bolted upright, flinging aside a cobweb-thin sheet and swinging her feet to the floor. "Two *hours?* Oh my God. Poor Reuben—he'll be frantic. He'll have called the police. And Jacinth, too—my sister."

She stood, or tried to, wobbled and then sank down again with a groan.

"I know they'll be worried." Marcus struggled beneath the weight of resignation. "I know that, and I'm sorry. But you'd better rest for a few minutes before you call. Before you report…whatever you decide to tell them."

His gaze locked onto hers and held it. But instead of the accusations, the curses, he'd expected, he saw something soften in her eyes.

"You're going to let me do that?" she asked.

He nodded. "Of course. Which is not to say I'm going to stick around and wait to be arrested."

She studied him for several moments. "Why were you out at the cemetery tonight? I mean, your camera *is* broken, right?"

"I was hoping you'd show up," he confessed. "I was hoping for a chance to catch you alone for a moment."

Her brows rose. "While I was leading a tour group?"

He smiled and shook his head. "I never said it was a *great* plan. But I was thinking maybe afterward you'd let me take you for a cup of coffee."

She rolled her eyes. "Oh, Reuben would've loved *that*."

"I was hoping your pit bull would look away for a minute."

"He's not my pit bull, he's my assistant. He's just a little... He used to be a cop, so he's naturally protective."

"Protective's one thing, but he looks like he enjoys ripping off heads just for fun."

"He grew up in a shack on Noble Street, smack up against the old projects," she said. "So what did you expect, a handshake and a warm welcome?"

Worry creased the smooth skin of her forehead, and moisture clumped her lower lashes. "Reuben may look like a tough guy, but he's going to be absolutely beside himself with me gone."

"Then call him," Marcus said. "Tell him you're all right."

Caitlyn looked worried. "You'll *really* let me do that?"

Marcus nodded solemnly. "I said I would. But if you can wait for just a minute, there's this one thing I have to show you first."

"This better not involve any body parts, or I promise you, I'll scream louder than you've ever heard a woman scream before." Her eyes sparkled like a honed blade. "In theater school, they always called me the girl with the made-for-horror-movie lungs."

"I remember from the cemetery." With another smile pulling at one corner of his mouth, he pulled the matchbook from his jeans pocket and tossed it to the bed. "That's the only thing I'm whipping out. Even if you beg me."

"Don't hold your breath," she murmured, picking up the matchbook.

"This morning in the cemetery, I accidentally grabbed this when I was gathering the stuff that fell out of my bag. I didn't notice it 'til later, after I'd already left your house."

She turned the matchbook cover, reading the advertising logo: *New Orleans After Dark Guided Tours.*

"I worked with Josiah Paine's company," she said, her voice trembling, "before I went out on my own."

"How does your old boss feel about the competition?"

Her gaze dropped, and she ran a corner of the sheet through her fingers, flicking the frayed hem with a chipped pink thumbnail. There was an unconscious sensuality in the small gesture, one that left Marcus too aware of their closeness in this cramped room, of the gulf of need that hollowed him out when he looked into her face.

In his mind's eye, the thin mattress grew feather-soft and cloud-thick. The worn cotton sheets rewove themselves from sumptuous threads of wine-rich silk. She lay back, her rain-tangled hair brushed to a fine sheen and splayed out against the heaps of fluffy pillows.

Looking away, he bit down hard on his tongue, desperate to bring both his imagination and his body to heel before she noticed and really did scream.

"Paine was furious about it," Caitlyn admitted in answer to his question. "But he never would've lost me if he'd kept his hands to himself."

Marcus's focus snapped back to her. "He put the moves on you?" He all but growled the question, a dark possessiveness roaring through his veins. If this Josiah Paine had touched her...

She shook her head, then lifted her hand toward the lump. "Ow—no. I didn't mean that. He just—he always had a temper. But one day he took it too far."

"How far?" Marcus ground out.

A delicate flush colored the exposed skin above her breasts. "One night he accused me of holding back tip money."

"What did he do?"

"The jerk shoved me, and I walked out. Started my own company, Villar-A1 Tours."

"Revenge?" he asked, as his own subconscious crept in that direction. Imagining himself pummeling a man he'd never met for a woman he hadn't even known at this time last night.

What the hell's wrong with me?

Picking up the matchbook and turning it around, she pressed her mouth into a grim line. "Turns out, it's not as sweet as I expected. Especially not if Josiah's insane enough to have killed poor Megan Lansky."

"That's the dead girl?"

Caitlyn told him about the student who had been reported missing, and how Megan had told her friends she was going on a cemetery tour. "The police thought about mine first, because of the resemblance and because I found her, but what if she went on one of Josiah's? He leads groups himself some nights—he's actually quite good—when one of the regular guides takes a night off or he's short-handed." She wrapped her arms around herself and added, "His employees tend to quit a lot. Or he gets mad and fires them. He's kind of famous for it. If I'd known when I first came to town…"

"Then the police are investigating him?"

"I doubt it. He seems to be a drinking buddy of some of the detectives. They acted like his temper's nothing but an old joke between—"

Cutting herself off, she began looking around, lifting the covers. "I really need to call Reuben. Where's my bag? My cell phone?"

"Sorry, but I didn't see them." Marcus picked up the receiver of the phone at his elbow. With a meaningful look, he passed it to her, and then forced himself to sit there, his jaw gritted, while he waited to find out if she would rain fresh hell down on his head.

CAITLYN FOUGHT TO LOOK AWAY and couldn't, held captive by the grim resolve on his face. Whatever she did or said, she realized Marcus wouldn't try to stop her. Wouldn't ask for help in keeping his involvement hidden, no matter what it cost him.

Though he'd cared enough for her, a virtual stranger, to bring her first the photo and then the matchbook from the crime scene, he expected nothing in return. Not even hope's ghost lived behind his storm-dark eyes.

Thunder murmured in the distance, followed by an answering frisson of awareness that sparked along her backbone. Alone inside this room, he could have done anything while she lay helpless. Could have but hadn't, only watched over her instead. Praying she would waken, he had told her.

Surely those details said something about the man he was. Perhaps more than the fact that he was avoiding the police.

Forcing herself to drop her gaze to dial and wait for an answer at the other end, she barely squeezed out a syllable of greeting before Reuben's worry blasted through the phone line.

"Are you hurt, girl? Where did you go? I've been goin' crazy lookin'. Called out half my buddies from the force to try to find you."

Her eyes stung at the pain she heard in his voice. Pain that Marcus had inflicted on a man who had shown her and her sister nothing but kindness since the day they had arrived in New Orleans.

"I'm sorry," she blurted. "So sorry you were frightened. What about the tour group? Everyone okay?"

"No one hurt, just shaken."

"And you?"

"You answer me first, *chère*," Reuben shot back.

"I'll be fine. I just…" She wanted to explain, but Marcus's regard, the weight of his bitter expectation, stopped her.

Looking into his dark eyes, she imagined she could almost hear him saying, *I'm already in the wind, so I don't give a damn what you do.* How long had it been since anyone had offered him the slightest support?

"This is so embarrassing," she said, astonished by the words that poured out. "When the lightning struck, I just—I panicked, Reuben. I don't know how else to explain it. I ran and ran before I understood what I was doing."

Marcus lifted dark brows in a question.

"I tripped," she added. "I must've hit my head. When I opened my eyes, it was pitch-dark. So I got up and started searching for you."

"What? Where *are* you, Caitlyn? Let me come and get you."

She slipped her hand over her eyes, hiding from her own lies. "I would've called before, but I lost my purse and my phone—"

"I've got 'em," Reuben told her. "But where the hell are—"

"That's great. Thanks, Reuben. I'm safe. Really." *Some trained actress,* she thought, recognizing the too-swift cadence and high pitch of her own panic. "I ran into a friend, and he's putting me in a cab. I'll be home soon. We can talk there."

"What friend? What's this number you're calling from? If you're in trouble, just say 'okay.'"

"I'm not in trouble, promise," she said lightly. "See you in a little bit. Bye."

"Caitlyn, don't hang—"

Guiltily, she replaced the receiver, handling it as carefully as she might a stick of dynamite. And ignoring it moments later when the phone rang and rang and rang.

MARCUS SAW SHE WAS STILL TREMBLING as he sat beside her on the bed and pulled her into his arms, unable to resist the tidal force of the impulse washing over him. Because against all odds, Caitlyn seemed to *see* him, the man behind the fugitive. She sighed against him, her body relaxing into his embrace.

It was more than anyone had done in years, and though he'd meant only to comfort her in her obvious distress, the result unleashed a passion that had him tipping back her head and slanting his mouth over hers. The shock of contact, the warm, full wetness of her mouth beneath his, sent raw desire spearing through him.

Yet he pulled back when she froze like a fawn. Pulled back to whisper, "You never need to fear me. To fear *this,* Caitlyn. Never…"

Half expecting her to scream or slap him, he waited, his breath held with the worry that four years punctuated only by the most fleeting and unsatisfying liaisons had cost him the ability to read a decent woman's cues. Had the connection he felt been a mirage formed out of loneliness and need?

Heat bloomed in her green eyes an instant before she closed them, leaning forward a bare fraction of an inch—but just enough.

In the gritty gloom of that small, cramped space, their kiss became all the world's light, focused to form one perfect, concentrated beam. A beam too bright to look at, too hot to bear for long.

Overwhelmed, he pulled his mouth from hers, only to dip his head to slide softer kisses along her neck, behind her ear, as, reverently, his hand skimmed along her ribs and waist, then found the sweet flare of her hip.

Her breaths were coming faster, as hard and quick as his own. Her soft fingertips feathered light caresses at his jawline.

With their bond a starved man's sustenance, Marcus could have feasted all night, feeding at the subtle notch beneath her pulsing throat, the willing heat of her mouth. But his impatient body had its own imperative, and before he knew what he was doing, he was untying and loosening the bodice of her peasant blouse.

Caitlyn pushed his hand away and sucked in a startled lungful of air. Jerking back, she fixed wide eyes on him, with passion, confusion and regret all playing staccato-swift through her expression.

"No." She slipped around him to clamber out of the bed. "No, I can't. This isn't me, for one thing. And Reuben's waiting, worried. I have to go. I *have* to."

With each word, she backed farther out of his reach.

"Caitlyn, it's all right," he said, though his body grieved her loss already. "There's no need to be upset."

Beyond listening, she turned from him, scrambling to unfasten the door's cheap chain and deadbolt.

"Don't go," he said. "I'll call a cab, like you told Reuben, and then I'll see you to it. You have a head injury, and this neighborhood's not safe for—"

But it was too late. Door swinging wide, Caitlyn blazed straight through it, not hesitating for an instant before she raced out into the sultry Crescent City night.

Chapter Five

Caitlyn slipped around a corner and ducked behind a trashcan, her heart a snare-quick drumbeat in her chest. She strained her ears to hear past the muted thump of a bass from somewhere nearby, her breath held until she heard footsteps pounding past. Marcus's footsteps, she was certain, even before she heard him calling her name. He sounded frantic, as worried as Reuben had been on the phone.

"What am I *doing?*" Her whisper echoed in an alley that reeked of garbage and a pungent smell she didn't dare risk considering too closely.

Though the rain had finally stopped, recriminations bounced back at her off wet brick and concrete: Reuben's and the detectives' warnings about Marcus, along with Jacinth's scolding that she was too quick to think the best of all those she encountered.

In every other way, you're brighter than anybody I know. In Caitlyn's memory, her sister's dark eyes gleamed with worry as she spoke. *But you're going to end up hurt if you keep dragging home strays and feeding strangers.*

Caitlyn sighed, realizing they'd all been right. She'd been dangerously naive, and kissing Marcus, a man who'd carried her beyond the help of Reuben and the police, proved it.

It proved, too, that she had gotten over her boyfriend in Ohio, who'd waited only three days after her move before texting that he guessed he wasn't cut out for long separations. Apparently he'd never been cut out for monogamy, either, according to her friends.

As devastated as she'd been, when she tried to picture Tony's face now, all she could see was Marcus, looking at her the way a lion looks at a gazelle. At the thought, her stomach quivered, though less with the fear she should be feeling than with the longing to call him back and offer herself up for his dinner.

Scowling at her own foolishness, she shook it off and moved on. As she crept back toward the streetlight, her head ached and her nausea reawakened.

A door swung open just ahead of her, blocking her escape from the alley. Loud music and cigarette smoke poured out of what she supposed must be a bar. An instant later, three men followed, each one bigger and louder than the last. With nothing taller than a small forest of discarded beer bottles for cover, she pressed her back against the wall and trusted to the shadows, her instincts warning her that she mustn't make a sound.

"Come on, how 'bout a taste here?" a jumpy outline wheedled. "Hook me up, bro—c'mon."

"Screw that," said a hulking figure. "You show the green and we'll deal."

"Ain't jerkin' us around, are you?" a third voice demanded. "'Cause if you're wastin' our time…"

A palpable threat hung in the air, and Caitlyn winced at the realization that she'd stumbled onto a drug deal. Icy terror twisting in her belly, she waited, holding her breath and praying they would finish their transaction quickly and ooze back inside. Oblivious as they were, it might have happened that way. And probably would have, had the edge of her skirt not caught a standing longneck and tipped the bottle over.

In the narrow space, the clatter of glass echoed loudly.

Caitlyn turned and raced toward the alley's opposite—and mercifully open—entrance.

Almost immediately, footsteps followed, accompanied by a man yelling, "Hey, sweetie! Come to Papa!" and a roar of coarse laughter.

And then more footsteps, hard on her heels, closing in with every step.

SWEAT WAS STREAMING down Marcus's face by the time he heard raised voices and men's shouts of excitement.

Tell me it's not Caitlyn. But he didn't allow the wish to slow him as he rushed toward the disturbance.

He was quick to realize he wasn't the only one hurrying to find out what was happening. In this seamy collection of strip clubs, last-call dives and liquor, lottery and po'boy sandwich shops with bars on every window, young men, transvestites and a few hard-looking women tended to mill around at midnight, many of them up for anything to ease their squalid boredom.

Especially the kind of "anything" involving a fresh-faced, beautiful young woman who clearly didn't belong.

By the lurid glow of a neon sign alternately flashing the messages *Girls, Hell Yes!* and *Clothes, Hell No!* he spotted at least a dozen lowlifes stumbling in the same direction. Not caring who he pissed off, Marcus pushed his way through oily clumps of humanity, parting them with such speed that only a handful of curses and one fist caught him—a glancing blow he barely felt.

His thrumming heart in his throat, he finally spotted Caitlyn as she threw open the door of an older silver car and called to the driver, "Oh, thank God it's you."

Marcus wanted to shout to her but didn't, deciding she was safer with a friend—even her damned pit bull—than she could ever be with him. The door closed and the car zoomed off, leaving him standing there alone, staring after her.

At least for the few seconds before the drunken bikers he'd shoved caught up.

"THANK YOU *SO* MUCH," Caitlyn repeated for the fifth time in five minutes. As little as she liked Mumbling Max Lafitte, she meant it. "I don't know what I would have done if you hadn't happened by."

He shot her an angry look, his balding scalp flashing as passing headlights bounced off the shine. "Reuben was going nuts looking for you out there. Where the hell have you been?"

It was the first thing he'd said to her as they proceeded toward her home.

"I got lost," she said simply. "Fell and hit my head."

Rather than asking if she was all right, he muttered, "Damned irresponsible, abandoning your tour group like that. Always figured you for flighty."

"You be sure and share that with your boss,"

she snapped. "Maybe he'll toss you some extra kibble."

"Bitch like you might like that better than I would."

Light strobed over his sneer, reminding her that he'd been there when the storm broke in the cemetery, horning in on her group and all too close by when someone had hit her on the head. Someone who had tried to drag her off in the confusion.

Chills erupted in an instant, with every fine hair on her body lifting. She could barely force words past the painful knot in her throat. Barely think of anything but throwing open the car door and bailing out into the street.

Could it really be him, a man she'd worked with for months?

"You know what?" She struggled to keep her voice steady. "There's a convenience store on the next corner. If you're going to be a jerk about it, just drop me off there and I'll call a cab."

His Adam's apple bobbed up and down, the same tic she'd noticed each time he'd crumbled beneath his boss's criticism. Passive-aggressive as Max might be, she reminded herself that he had always backed down when confronted."Sorry you got hurt," he said sourly.

The car glided past the store, which Caitlyn noticed had closed since she'd last been by.

"But not for calling me a bitch?" she pressed. "What exactly is your problem with me, Max?"

He flicked a sullen glance at her. "You heard Josiah. Always harping on me about how I was the veteran, but *you* were the one bringin' in the money."

"If he hadn't been riding you about that, it would have been something else. You know him. But this business lately with you crowding out my tour groups, this is starting to feel personal. And I've been nice to you from day one, and you know it."

He shrugged. "Let's just say I don't like you and leave it at that."

"I don't think I will. I'm asking you again, Max. Either explain it, or quit bothering me and we'll never have to speak again."

He turned onto Esplanade Avenue, his clenched fists jerking the wheel so abruptly that her head throbbed in protest.

"You really can't imagine why I'd hate some pretty blonde thing—a damned Yankee, at that— who comes swishing her tail into *my* business and showing me up? Acting like she's entitled to everything I've worked for." His voice dropped to a low growl. "You're no better than your mama."

An electric jolt seared its way up her spine. "You knew my mother when she lived here?"

"Everybody knew Sophie Villaré. Worst

damned tease in town. And that daddy of yours... Never met a problem he didn't figure he could solve with his fists—including stealing another man's woman when he took a fancy to her. No surprise he ended up dead." The look Max shot her boiled with resentment. "And I'll tell you straight out, I'm not one bit sorry, either."

A memory splashed over Caitlyn's vision, an image of Detective Lorna Robinson rearranging letters to spell out V-I-L-L-A-R-E. Though he must be in his late fifties or maybe even older, could Max Lafitte be working with an older woman...perhaps even his own mother? Could he have somehow convinced her to play the role of Eva Rill to help him avenge some wrong, real or imagined, her parents had inflicted on him?

In the light of day, she wouldn't even consider such a wild possibility. But closed inside this car, inside the black bubble of Max's anger and frustration, the idea didn't seem too far-fetched to imagine.

"That's my house—right there," Caitlyn squeaked out. "Thanks again for the ride."

When he didn't answer, she held her breath, unable to bear the tension of not knowing whether he would slow down or zoom past.

Chapter Six

He had grown into the kind of man to take care of his mother, to move her with him to a decent house where the dolls could finally have a room all their own. His mother left her men behind, the men who paid to touch her but sometimes crept into her son's room, some of them so filthy drunk or thoroughly evil that they didn't care or notice that the dolls were bearing witness.

None of that mattered now. All that was important was the way he'd grown into a good man, the kind of man any decent woman should be proud to go home with. The kind of man they had no business—no damned right—to say no to, much less shriek and run away from.

So what if he still liked to sit in the center of his doll room, thinking? And so what if the blue and brown and hazel glass eyes that smiled back at him had all been changed to green?

WISHING FOR SOME ICE, Marcus settled for aspirin to cut the ache of the handful of bruises he had picked up. At least he had the satisfaction of knowing that the one man drunk enough to ignore his glare would be spending the rest of the evening in an E.R. instead of making trouble.

Marcus smoothed antibiotic ointment over his scraped knuckles and flexed his stiffening fingers. Finding them in working order, he used his prepaid cell phone to make a call he'd put off for far too long.

Even after ten rings, Isaiah Jericho didn't answer. Dread pooled in Marcus's gut. Would this be the night things fell apart? The night the old man didn't wake up?

He clicked off, his hands clenching. But there was no one else to call, so out of desperation, he tried his former mentor once again. "Come on, Isaiah. Pick up. You're the one who's always saying how you can never sleep."

He could almost hear the complaint. *Another of the curses of old age.*

But not the worst of it for Isaiah, they both knew. For a man whose renown in the field of photography had eclipsed even the popularity of Ansel Adams in his heyday, confinement to his home with no new images to photograph and no new vistas to explore was torture.

For the past four years his former protégé had been the frail old man's ticket out of hell, and the incredible gift of Isaiah's forgiveness and earning power had proved to be Marcus's salvation. How could he ever pay for his brother Theo's care if their partnership was over?

On the thirteenth ring, someone answered, and the sounds of Isaiah's sputtered curses had Marcus sighing with relief.

"Sorry I disturbed you."

"There had better be someone dead," the old man told him. "I was on the edge of the Grand Canyon, all that light and beauty laid out before me like a king's feast."

Marcus understood at once that Isaiah meant he'd been dreaming, and he felt the pain of longing in the eighty-six-year-old's fading voice.

"I can't afford to wait around here," Marcus said. "I need to get out of New Orleans or I'm going to end up being picked up for questioning—or worse."

He briefly explained the situation, though he glossed over the specifics. Especially the temporary insanity that had prompted him to put Caitlyn in his car and take her to his motel.

But Isaiah didn't seem to hear what he was saying. "You can't leave," he insisted. "Not until you've finished the series. Until *we've* finished it."

Though Marcus actually shot the photos, Isaiah was the one who'd adapted the techniques he'd perfected over many years to create a limited-edition series of art-quality prints on the finest papers. These he sold to collectors eager for the "final works" of a master.

Marcus regretted the deception and mourned the death of his chance to build his own reputation. But with his brother's care running into the thousands each month and no way to legitimately make that much money, he couldn't imagine what other choice he had.

"There are other cemeteries," Marcus told Isaiah. "Other interesting statues I can shoot."

"Not without your new lens. You'll have it in two days, express mail, if you're still there to get it. Besides, I need more shots of your dawn angel at noon, at dusk, by moonlight—in every kind of light and weather you can manage. It has to be the same one you sent by email. I need her. Only her…"

The hunger in the old man's words painted an image of Caitlyn Villaré in Marcus's mind. Probably because he'd met her at the exact moment he had snapped the photo that had immediately captured Isaiah's imagination.

First one angel, then another…

"Maybe I can risk swinging back through town in a few months," he suggested, imagining that Caitlyn might even be glad to see him, once the police caught Megan Lansky's killer.

There was a long pause, during which Marcus

heard only the electric hum of Isaiah's oxygen compressor. Finally the old man said, "We don't have a few months. Or I don't, anyway."

"You're sure this time?"

"Dead certain, if you'll forgive the pun. The doctors have said only weeks, without the surgery. But that would likely kill me outright, and anyway, I'm tired, Marcus. And I'm ready."

Shock detonated in cold waves through Marcus's chest, though he should have known this day was coming. Should have prepared himself to deal with the emotions, or at the very least the impact on his family.

"I'm sorry," he said, hollowed out by how weak the small words felt, like frail sparrows hurled into a hurricane. Even more uselessly, he added, "What can I do?"

"Finish this…this series, and let me unveil it under both our names. Admit to the deception— that I took what wasn't mine."

"No." Pain forked through Marcus's skull. "You were *helping* me, not stealing. Saving my ass and my family's."

"I *was* using you. Extending my day in the sun because I couldn't bear the darkness. But the shadow's closing in now. I'm running out of time to make peace with it."

Marcus shut his eyes and pressed his fingers to his throbbing forehead. How could he thank a man who'd recognized a poor, orphaned kid's potential, who'd shaped it into something that would forever nourish his soul?

Voice shaking, he said, "Then use me one more time, Isaiah. I'm going to get those photos for you, and they're going to be *your* legacy. Just hang in there for a few days. You've got to stay alert and sharp so you can work your magic, do you hear me?"

From the other end, there was no answer.

"Do you hear me, you stubborn old man? We're going to do this one last time. Together. You have my word."

As SHE MADE COFFEE THE NEXT MORNING, Caitlyn tiptoed on bare feet through the kitchen, trying not to wake Reuben. She hated the guilt nestled like a burning coal against her breastbone, the sick feeling she had at the idea of reigniting last night's argument with him.

But Sinister, who didn't give a fur-ball about the problems of mere mortals, brushed up against her naked legs and started demanding breakfast. Caitlyn tried to shush him while quickly rummaging for an offering to appease the hairy tyrant.

She set down his dish and changed his water, but as she straightened, she saw Reuben standing in the doorway.

"Sorry the beast woke you. Want some coffee?" She tugged nervously at the hem of the T-shirt she had pulled on over a pair of shorts.

Despite the brightness of her tone, the look on his face warned that he no more bought her story now than he had last night.

"Sure, and I'll have a big, heapin' bowl of truth with it this morning." He ran his fingers through his salt-and-pepper hair, the set of his jaw pure aggravation. "You ready to serve it up yet?"

Though Caitlyn hadn't grown up with a dad of her own, ever since Reuben had introduced himself at their grandmother's funeral, she had come to realize what it must be like, wanting both to please and rebel against the same man. It was an odd way of looking at her own assistant, but considering the difference in their ages and his connection to the father she couldn't remember, she couldn't think of him in any other way.

Her stomach twisting with the same apprehension that had kept her up half the night, she admitted, "You're right, Reuben. There *was* a lot more to the story than I told you."

He allowed her a tight nod before taking out a pair of mugs and pouring both of them some coffee. Perhaps as a peace offering, he stirred some vanilla soymilk into Caitlyn's without comment, though he normally had to remark about how plain old cow juice was good enough for him.

Once both of them were sitting at the table, Caitlyn realized she couldn't put it off another moment. "This lump I have on my head—I'm pretty certain someone hit me after the lightning strike."

"*Hit* you? So you *didn't* trip and fall." In his voice, she heard his unspoken *I knew it.*

"I was knocked out, so I don't remember," she said. "But I have reason to believe that someone tried to carry me off."

"Somebody attacked you in the cemetery? The same cemetery where a girl who looked like you was found dead?" He stood and paced, unable to physically contain the energy crackling through his huge frame. "Why the hell would you keep somethin' like that from me? From the police?"

"A friend fought off my attacker," she said. "He got me out of there."

"What kind of *friend* would do that without taking you to the hospital or calling the cops? I need to know this idiot's name and address."

"I told you last night, I can't say."

"You mean you *won't.*" After studying her intently, he blinked and snapped his fingers. "It's that guy who claimed his name is Marcus, isn't it? He showed up yesterday with that picture, and he was there again last night, wasn't he?"

She dropped her gaze. Despite her acting background, lying had never come naturally to her. But the idea of admitting she'd protected, even kissed, Marcus had heat rushing to her face.

And the dreams she'd had about him last night redoubled her discomfort.

"Never mind an answer. I can see it in your blush," Reuben grumbled. "Now tell me, what lies did that piece of garbage fill your head with?"

Before she could stop herself, the words burst out. "He wasn't lying. He was trying to help me."

"*Help* you?" Reuben shook his head. "He's trying to help himself *to* you. There's a big difference."

Moisture hazed her vision. "I know that, and I realize how it must sound. But if you talked to him, you'd see what he's like."

"He doesn't want me or anybody else talkin' to him. Take it from an old cop—this creep's zeroed in on you. Sought you out when you were alone, then found himself an opportunity to cut you from the herd, maybe even by hitting you over the head himself." Reuben pounded his fist on the counter. "You're damn lucky you're alive, *chère*. Unlike poor Megan Lansky."

"Marcus didn't murder anybody." *Much less*

replace his victim's eyes with painted glass and dress her in a blond wig.

Shuddering with revulsion, Caitlyn wanted to get up, to run upstairs and lock herself in her room like a child, but Reuben's sad gaze pinned her in place.

"How can you be so sure?" he asked. "And how could I think anything else?"

This time his point sank in, and her doubt leaked from the wound.

When she said nothing, Reuben picked up the phone. "I don't know why you lied to me about this, but you're going to explain it. If not to me, then to the detectives. I'm calling them right now, and believe me, they are going to want some answers."

WHEN THE HEAT WOKE CAITLYN, she found herself slumped in a rocking chair beneath a ceiling fan that barely stirred the languid air. She rose stiffly, her legs sticking to the wood, and rubbed her damp neck, then checked the clock beside her bed.

Five-fifteen already? She would have sworn she had only sat down and closed her eyes for a few minutes, not for more than three hours.

Cursing the broken air-conditioning, she showered, allowing the cool water to sluice over her, but nothing could wash away the prickling of anxiety that had sent her upstairs in the first place.

Had the police found and questioned—even arrested—Marcus since she'd spoken to them? Was he in an interview room or a jail cell right now, wishing he had never met her, much less saved her life?

Which he *had*. She still believed that, regardless of anything Reuben or the increasingly exasperated detectives told her. She knew she'd seen concern in his eyes, felt tenderness in his touch.

As she dried herself and pulled on a clean cotton sundress, fresh doubts needled. Had she really made the right choice, telling the police the name of the motel where Marcus had taken her?

But what else could she do, with Detective Robinson staring a hole into her conscience, saying, *It's my sworn duty to give Megan Lansky's family justice and to help them make sense of the terrible things done to their daughter. Don't you think they deserve at least that much, Caitlyn? Don't you want this killer, whoever he is, caught?*

Downstairs, she stood in front of the open refrigerator door for too long, not wanting to eat but realizing she'd been too upset to think of food all day, and there would be another tour this evening. Sinister, who thought of little besides eating all the time, yowled up at her, so she paused to feed him a can of Prissy Friskers, the only cat food on the planet he would deign to eat.

Wrinkling her nose at the smelly fish, she made herself a meal of a sliced nectarine and yogurt with a handful of chopped walnuts. Halfway through it, she heard Reuben talking in the room they had set up as an office.

Since he frequently took reservations for upcoming tours, she at first thought nothing of it. But as she took a few more bites, she made out two distinct words, "Complete bull," sounding clipped and angry. Was he arguing with someone on the phone or in the house?

Wiping her napkin across her mouth and tossing it in the trashcan, she went to investigate. Reaching the partly open door, she lifted her hand with the intent of rapping lightly to let him know she was there.

Instead, she froze as she caught what he was saying.

"…no *publicity* stunt. I don't give a damn how strapped she is for money or what your *good buddy* Josiah Paine's been telling you. Caitlyn Villaré wouldn't make up this stuff, and she'd never be involved in murder."

The food she had just eaten threatened to come up. Was someone—most likely Detective Davis, who had spoken so highly of Paine's generosity—actually suggesting she might be involved with...

No. The idea was ridiculous.

Caitlyn nudged the door wider, but Reuben's stiffened back was to her, the phone to his ear as he shook his head.

"Sure you know your job, Detective, but you don't know this girl. Real sweet kid, for one of those crunchy-granola drama types."

Though at another time she might have smiled at Reuben's description, tears sprang to her eyes at the fierceness of his defense, especially considering how she had initially lied to him about her disappearance.

"She's naive, that's all," he insisted. "You've got a better chance of busting a Disney princess for a criminal plot than this gal."

Smile fading, Caitlyn leaned against the door. The hinges creaked, and Reuben turned, eyes widening when he saw her standing there.

"Listen, Davis," he said into the phone. "I gotta go. Thanks for the update."

Once he hung up, he turned to her and said, "I thought you were still sleeping. So how much of that did you hear?"

She willed herself to stand taller. "When you and Jacinth call me *naive,* what I really hear is *stupid. Helpless. Someone who can't be trusted with the pointy scissors.*"

His brows shot up, and he snorted. "You want to get your knickers in a twist about *that?* When you've got a killer stalkin' you, and Detective Davis is thinkin' you might be part of some sick scheme to buy publicity?"

She winced at the reminder. "Thanks loads for making me feel petty." Then she took a deep breath and willed herself to calm down. "Seriously, I really do appreciate your vouching for me."

"Tell you what. Next time, I'll let him know you're a hardened gun moll, if that makes you feel any better." He followed with a wink to show her he was joking.

"I don't understand. Why would they suspect *me?*"

He shrugged. "First off, you were the only witness to the old lady comin' to your place before dawn. They've been circulating the picture, but nobody's recognized her."

"She wasn't a figment of my imagination. They saw the photo from the cemetery."

"I told him it was her, too, the same lady from our tour the night before. But he's tellin' me somebody should be able to ID her."

Caitlyn shook her head. "Maybe she doesn't normally look that way. The black dress, the hat with the veil—the costume misdirects the audience, makes the actress the character in their minds."

"I love it when you talk theater to me." A sardonic smile tilted one corner of his mouth before he grew serious. "And you could be right about that. But there are other factors, like the fact that you were awfully slow to admit what really happened last night."

"I bet your detective buddy has been talking to Josiah," she said. "Maybe collecting a few donations for the widows and orphans."

The implication hung in the air only a moment before Reuben's face went red. "That's what you're sayin' now, that the detective's corrupt? That he's just another dirty cop in this town?"

"No, no. I didn't mean to imply that your friend—"

"You damned well better not be, not when there's good reason for the cops to look at every possibility. Especially with the media breathin' down their necks."

Uncomfortable with his anger, she seized on the change of subject. "The media?"

His anger faded into a sigh. "I feel bad breakin' this to you, but some hotshot investigative reporter got hold of a photo of Megan Lansky with the blond wig, and then saw a picture of you leaving the crime scene. Didn't take long for him to put two and two together—probably with the help of a leak out of the P.D."

"Then it's—it's in the *news* that this is tied to me?" Caitlyn's knees wobbled as the room began to spin around her.

Reuben grabbed the rolling chair from the desk and guided her to sit. "Sorry, *ma chère,* but it's the lead story on every station. They're runnin' pictures of you off the website, in your costume, makin' a big thing out of your—" he sketched quotes with his fingers "—'flair for drama.'"

He pointed to a small TV, which was playing on mute. "I've been fielding calls for interviews all day."

Caitlyn leaned forward, holding her head in her hands.

Reuben asked, "I should've made you see a doctor. I should have—"

She forced herself to look up. "I'm okay, it's just—"

Her jaw loosened as she recognized the fleshy red face on the screen. A clearly furious man in his late fifties. "Oh, my Lord, is that Josiah?"

When Reuben reached for the power button, she said, "Not off—turn it up, please."

She heard him sigh, but he did as she asked, and sure enough, Josiah Paine was mopping sweat from his face with a handkerchief and standing in front of the freshly painted sign advertising New Orleans After Dark Tours.

Sneering, he said, "Ungrateful and manipulative—that's what Caitlyn Villaré was. Using me to get just enough experience to stab me in the back after I fired her for... Let's just say that in a mostly cash-based business, it's important to have totally trustworthy employees."

Face burning, she shot up from her chair. "That lying— I can't believe he would—would *use* this situation to—"

Choked by angry tears, she couldn't even get the rest out. Especially not with thoughts about the matchbook Marcus had found dominating her thoughts. Not that the police had seemed the slightest bit interested when she had passed on word of his discovery.

Reuben's knees creaked as he squatted beside her. "Paine's just a small man with a big mouth. Everybody who matters knows that."

"No. *Everybody* doesn't. What they think they know about me now is that I'm some kind of conniving thief who's wrapped up in this murder. Even the police think so. You said it yourself."

"They're just frustrated that your...*friend*— this Marcus fella—slipped away before the uniforms got to the motel."

Her heart lightened for a moment. *I hope you*

get away from here, Marcus. Heaven knows, I wish I could.

But there was no escape from her dilemma. She didn't even have a car to flee in, since there had been no money to replace her clunker when it finally cratered a few months earlier.

With this public flogging, there would be no way for her to make her living, either. She couldn't possibly lead tour groups while being hounded by reporters. Tears filled her eyes at the unfairness of it and the impossibility of explaining that she, too, was a victim in this—that she might be the next one murdered.

The newscast cut to another story, leaving the viewer one last glimpse of the raw hatred in Paine's watery blue eyes. And leaving her to wonder, had he merely seized on this opportunity to trash her?

Or was he obsessed enough with avenging his wounded pride that he would kill an innocent to set this nightmare into motion?

Chapter Seven

Two more long days slipped past Marcus, days he counted off in newscasts watched in different motel rooms each night. Late each afternoon, he presented an Indiana driver's license—a convincing fake in the name of Michael David Johns—at the city's main post office in the hope that his general delivery package had finally arrived.

It came as a relief to claim it, to finally have the means to complete his photo series and put New Orleans behind him.

And put her behind me, too, he thought, understanding that his dangerous fixation on Caitlyn Villaré needed to come to an end.

Everywhere, he saw her. On TV and in memory, in his dreams each night. In every golden glimpse of blond he spotted in a restaurant or on the street. He had even turned around this afternoon, convinced he'd seen her leaving the post office as he entered.

He resisted the urge to run after the retreating

figure, to tear the sunglasses from her face and ask if she was crazy to be out on her own. For one thing, it was none of his damned business if she decided to risk attracting the attention of her stalker or reporters. For another, it wouldn't be her, just as it hadn't been every other time he'd looked.

Retreating to his car, he cranked the engine and turned the AC on high. Instead of driving off, he kept the Chevy in Park and pulled his camera from its case.

If the lens was indeed the only part that had broken, he could quickly replace it and begin taking his photos. Within a few days—maybe less, if he could slip in and out of the cemetery without attracting undue attention—he could leave this city. Maybe he would drive west into Texas and then drift south across the border.

Surely, in Mexico, he would see far fewer blondes. And with time and enough tequila, maybe he would even stop dreaming about the taste of Caitlyn's kiss, the silken heat of her skin. Once he could eat and sleep again, he would be able to wrap his mind around the problem of how to earn enough money to keep Theo in caregivers and medication.

Those were his only real responsibilities. Caitlyn had both the police and what amounted to a full-time bodyguard to keep her safe from what-ever lunatic was bent on doing her harm.

Swallowing hard, he removed the new lens from the packing material to check it. "Let this take care of the problem so I can be on my way," he whispered.

While his heart and body breathed an alto-gether different prayer.

ONCE CAITLYN FINISHED mailing the package to her sister, she hurried out of the post office toward the spot where Natalie was waiting in the car. Her friend had wanted to come inside with her, but with no spaces available, Natalie had been forced to park illegally, and she wasn't about to have her Honda towed for the second time this month.

Reuben would have had a fit, but Caitlyn was thrilled to escape what she thought of as pro-tective custody, to pretend, even for a few short minutes, that she wasn't being hunted by both the media and a killer. Besides that, she felt safe in such a busy public place, with plenty of wit-nesses and a huge pair of sunglasses hiding her face. More of a theatrical disguise than a real one, she knew, but at times like this a pinch of self-delusion was good for the soul.

When she came out, Natalie and her car were both gone. A police officer on bike patrol was clearly the reason why. Frowning, Caitlyn jogged out of the officer's line of sight and toward the corner, where she hoped to spot the small red car somewhere along the street.

Instead, she was the one spotted—by Josiah Paine, who came striding down the sidewalk, looking bent on adding her to his collection of stuffed creatures.

A big man, he was already sweating through a shirt that looked more Hawaii than New Orleans, his fleshy face as red and angry as it had been on the news.

"You!" he shouted, pointing straight at her face.

Though her heart was pounding wildly, she didn't give an inch. "Careful, Josiah. You push me here, in front of witnesses, and you can be sure I'll press charges."

"You backstabbing little bitch. You tell my pals I killed that college girl? What kind of sick—I oughta sue your ass for libel." Spittle flew as he closed in, looming over her.

She hated the fear crowding against her lungs, the quivering of her knees. Hated it so much, it made her furious. "You mean slander, don't you? Either way, you're out of luck. I didn't tell them you killed anyone. But they asked me about enemies, so of course, your name came up."

"You have a hell of a lot of nerve—"

"Oh, come off it." She noticed several people stopping to watch. She hoped at least one of them would shout for the bike-patrol officer if things got out of hand. "After the way you trashed me on the news, you can't go around acting like it's a big secret you can't stand me."

"They took me in. You know that? Hauled me in for questioning, in front of God and everybody."

She lifted a palm. "And yet you're still walking free."

"That's right, Caitlyn." Leaning even closer, he dropped his voice to speak in quiet tones more terrifying than all his shouting. "I'm walking free. Guess you didn't realize I've got friends in the department. Friends in the department and even better friends outside it. The kind of friends ready to do any favor to help a buddy settle an old grudge."

INSIDE HIS CAR, Marcus put the camera back together and found all its functions seemingly intact. Still, he would have to test it, then check the quality of the shots on his laptop.

He could do it here, in the central business district. But looking up, he noticed sunlight forking through the clouds that had been building all day. Immediately, he recognized conditions with the potential to highlight his dawn angel to breathtaking effect.

Before the decision even registered, he found

himself driving to the cemetery, his mind filling with the statue, which seemed to spin on some hidden axis. Or perhaps the angel *was* the axis, with the whole world whirling around her. By the time he found a place to park and walked the two blocks to the cemetery gates, he had envisioned her from every angle, in every kind of light and weather.

In the steaming summer heat, the streets of the city of the dead were nearly empty, save for a cloud of industrious mosquitoes and three die-hard tourists, middle-aged women who fanned themselves with brochures as they argued over where to go next.

Keeping his distance, Marcus took a few shots of the angel but soon found himself distracted by a heap of wilting flowers, a makeshift memorial left to honor the murder victim Caitlyn had stumbled over three days earlier.

Remembrance dropped him to one knee, drove him like a nail back into the moment. To the old woman hidden behind the tomb, only spotted later in his photo. To the dead woman in the blond wig, to the living version who had knocked him down.

Caitlyn...

"Marcus?"

At the sound of her voice, he stiffened, wondering whether an obsession could burn so bright and hot, it left behind a residue of madness.

"Marcus, are you all right?" she asked, and he turned toward her, drawn irresistibly to the possibility she might be real.

Rising, he took in her dark glasses, the same dark glasses he had spotted at the post office earlier. Same gauzy turquoise dress, too, only now she'd tucked her hair up beneath a wide-brimmed straw hat. Her lips were trembling as she stared, her body as taut as a drawn bowstring. He half expected her to fly away at his approach.

"You followed me from the post office," he accused her. As much as he had longed to see her, he couldn't shake the feeling that there would be consequences, repercussions he could ill afford. "You came *here*—alone—after everything that's happened?"

"Please, I had to see you." Her words touched him like a cool breeze. "Besides, my friend's waiting in her car. If I'm not back in five minutes, she'll call the police."

He wanted to remind her of how many things could go wrong within the space of a few seconds. But she shook her head and pulled off her sunglasses, revealing reddened eyes.

"Don't lecture me," she pleaded. "I couldn't help it. I needed to talk to someone who'd believe me. So when I saw your car..."

He frowned, concern edging past his caution. "What's happened?"

She nodded. "Just before I spotted you leaving the post office, Josiah Paine threatened me out on the sidewalk."

Marcus's anger flared like a struck match. "What did he say?"

"It's more what he implied."

"Which was…?"

"That his cop buddies would look the other way while his criminal friends settled his scores for him. And I'm absolutely sure he meant me. He's furious and embarrassed that the police took him in for questioning."

Marcus sucked in a deep breath to clear his head. Though he was tempted to track Paine down and squash him like the fat maggot he was, there had to be a more rational solution. "If he was brought in, then he can't be friends with the whole force. Report what he said, and keep reporting it until you find someone who'll listen."

"He'll just claim I made it up."

"There were no witnesses?"

She shook her head, her voice trembling with frustration. "People saw us together, but no one was close enough to hear what he said. For once in his life, he was careful not to yell."

He started to reach for her, but then, thinking

better of it, dropped his hand to his thigh. "He really scared you, didn't he?"

"That's the strange part. I've been yelled at by him so often, I've learned to mostly tune him out. But when he looked at me the way he did and went so quiet, I saw something in his eyes I've never seen before—something that made me think about what was done to Megan Lansky."

"You're going to have to tell somebody. The police, your pit bull—someone who can help you." As much as it pained him to admit it, he forced himself to say, "Because however much I want to, I can't be the one to fix this. I have to leave here, Caitlyn. I have to leave here very soon."

When more of her hair slid free, she pulled off the hat and, with a nervous flutter, fanned her face with its broad brim. "I know you can't help me. But at least you don't treat me like some melodramatic airhead."

"First of all, you'd be crazy not to be upset after everything you've been through." Finally giving in to the need to touch her, he took her hand and stroked his thumb across her knuckles. "And believe me, I have never seen you as an airhead, not for a single moment."

Leaning closer, he skimmed his lips over her soft cheek and whispered into her ear, "You're the woman that I dream of. Or do you need a reminder of that, Caitlyn?"

When he felt her shiver, he kissed her sweet mouth, the pleasure arcing hot and wild between them. He wanted to go on kissing her forever, to forget where they were standing, to forget that he was leaving any day. To forget he was on the run, a man about to lose his livelihood. A fugitive with no damned business feeling this way about an innocent.

Caitlyn pushed at his chest, and as they broke apart, he saw both desire and pain flash through her green eyes. Shaking her head, she told him, "I can't do this, Marcus. I have to go now, before Natalie gets nervous, but first I need—I want—to say I'm really sorry."

"Sorry for what?"

"For running out the way I did the other night." Moisture gleamed in her eyes. "And for telling the police where you were staying."

"You told them?" He reminded himself that he shouldn't be surprised, much less disappointed. It wasn't as if she owed him any loyalty.

She nodded. "The detectives said they had to rule you out so they could move on with their investigation. They said I was holding things up, keeping information from them."

Dangerous as the police attention was, a rush of pleasure had him smiling. "You held out?"

She nodded. "Until the morning, and I can tell you, they weren't happy, especially Detective Davis."

"I've been following the news," he said. "It sounds like they don't have anything, not really."

"As of this morning, they do." Replacing her hat, she pushed a drooping strand beneath it. "Reuben heard, from one of the cops he used to work with."

"Heard what?"

She glanced back over her shoulder and then shook her head. "I'd better call Natalie. I don't want her freaking out or reporting me to Reuben."

Before he could say anything, she'd pulled a phone from her loosely woven shoulder bag and pushed a number.

"Hey, Nat, I need another favor. I met up with my friend—mmm-hmm, yeah, the really hot guy from outside the post office." Caitlyn slid a grin toward Marcus. "We're going out for dinner. Think you can cover for me if I tell Reuben you and I went for a sandwich?"

She listened for a minute before nodding. "I know I owe you. Tell you what, free babysitting for Kylie next time you want to go out with *your* new guy. All right, any *Saturday*. Thank you— and thanks again for the ride. I was going crazy stuck inside that sweatbox of a house."

After finishing her call, she sent a quick text message—to her pit bull, Marcus supposed—before she slid the phone back inside her bag. And when she smiled at him, he realized how wrong he had been to imagine a lifeless statue made of stone, however beautiful, as his world's axis.

This woman was far more compelling. A work of art he could study for a century and never tire of.

But the gift of her beauty was nothing compared to the offering she had just made of her safety. By sending her friend home as she had, casting off her lifeline, she was telling him that she had willingly chosen to trust a man who couldn't even offer her his entire name.

Or could he?

Heart pounding, he thrust out his hand, a hand callused from the menial labor he sometimes resorted to in order to send his sister extra money for their brother's care. Shaking Caitlyn's hand, he said, "Marcus Le Carpentier. I'm very glad to meet you."

Popping the lens cap on his camera, he took another risk by saying, "Let me make an honest woman of you and take you to dinner."

And then she gave him yet another gift by smiling and following him back to his car.

*S*HE THOUGHT SHE COULD *escape him, going off with Villaré again, with his shining blue-black hair and dark eyes, and cocky self-assurance.*

As much a threat as ever, except...

Wasn't Micah Villaré dead? Hadn't he been dead, and his stolen bride, Sophie, gone, forever?

A buzzing like a cloud of flies began in his head, making him wish he were back within the windowless confines of the air-conditioned doll room, where everything still made sense, where none of the green-eyed girls laughed at him. Where no one had ever run off with a handsome and entitled bastard.

Where he never felt the need to choke, to shake, to force them...a need that came roaring upon him, unstoppable, unbearable, until it was finally quenched.

Chapter Eight

As if by mutual agreement, Caitlyn and Marcus focused on the mundane, from the selection of a small, dark hideaway known to locals for its excellent food, to the location of a parking space and their choice of entrées. They spoke of nothing of consequence, limiting their conversation to the hot and yeasty croissants with honeyed butter served as an appetizer, the meal that arrived too soon—the rare strip steak Marcus had ordered, along with Caitlyn's roasted tomato caprese salad, which thrilled her to the depths of her vegetarian soul.

When the waiter came with the dessert tray, Marcus smiled and insisted, and Caitlyn took him up on it, choosing a sinfully delicious crème brûlée that she laughingly claimed was larger than her first apartment.

They shared, until Marcus told her he was full and watched while she used the edge of her spoon to crack off the last bit of the mouthwatering burnt-sugar topping. Scooping it up with the final bite of the vanilla custard beneath, she closed her eyes, practically purring with pleasure.

When she looked up, he was grinning. "I have to tell you, Caitlyn, seeing that was worth the price of dinner."

Her face heated as a new hunger in his dark eyes told her that he was imagining her pleasure in a far more private context. She struggled to keep her mind from following, from imagining him clothed only in a sheet and looking at her that way.

Her spoon slipped from her fingers, chiming as it struck the crystal water glass. Mercifully, the waiter arrived and poured them each another cup of smooth, rich coffee.

Marcus's grin faded to a wistful smile. "I've almost forgotten what it feels like, enjoying a delicious dinner in the company of a beautiful woman."

She wanted to protest, to make some joke to ease the sadness that had come over him. But before she could, it infected her mood, too.

As wonderful as it had felt, pretending they were two different people in different circumstances, she knew as well as he did that their time was fleeting and they couldn't afford to waste it playing at this impossible flirtation.

"It hasn't hit the news yet," she said, "but

Reuben told me the police have come across several similar killings from the late eighties. Four dead prostitutes with blond wigs and those horrible green glass eyes."

"Here in New Orleans?"

She nodded. "The cases went cold—for one thing, no one was exactly clamoring to solve the murders of streetwalkers—and when the killings stopped, everyone forgot. Until Megan Lansky."

"So they think it could be the same killer...? That would definitely make him—"

"In his forties or fifties, maybe even older."

The conversation paused as the waiter discreetly dropped the check at Marcus's elbow. She reached for her purse—and the one credit card she hadn't maxed out—but he waved her off and paid the bill, along with a generous tip, in cash.

"That age range would fit Josiah Paine," Caitlyn continued, once they left the restaurant. "And one of his tour guides, too, a man named Max Lafitte. He's been mad at me since I outshone him in front of Paine, and he's still holding on to some kind of grudge against my parents."

She told him about the ride the man had given her the night she'd run from the hotel. Shivering, she hugged herself as she finished.

They walked back toward where they'd left the car, and he took her arm, guiding her around the places where the sidewalk had been tipped or broken by the roots of the huge old trees lining the mostly residential street. Soon they stepped into the shadow of an old church that looked more like a castle.

Marcus stopped, murmuring, "Excuse me," and pulled the camera he'd brought with him from its case.

While she waited, he photographed a detail she never would have noticed, a stained glass window glowing from the inside, lit by the setting sun behind the building.

"You got your camera fixed?" she asked. "Or did you have to buy a new one?"

"Just the lens." He quickly put away the camera.

Remembering the stunning shots she'd seen on his computer in his motel room, she suspected he might be a travel photographer. But how could he work for any legitimate publication while on the run from the law? How would he collect his fees?

Clearly distracted, he started toward the car again. "I was just thinking about something. Wondering how that old woman fits into all this."

Caitlyn shook her head. "She was playing up the creep factor, dressing all in black and giving me a number that turned out to belong to a local mortuary."

"You said she claimed she'd lost the ring the victim was found wearing."

"A priceless heirloom, that's what she told me, but it turned out to be a piece of inexpensive costume jewelry, just part of some plan to lure me to the cemetery that morning."

"To kill you, too? Is that what you think?"

"Maybe. But I took Reuben with me, and you were there, too."

"Speaking of your pit b—your *assistant*—I should get you back home." Regret deepened in Marcus's eyes. "You really need to talk to him about what happened with Paine."

Her throat tightened as she realized that their interlude was over. That in the end it had solved nothing but only intensified her need to be with him again.

Shaking her head, she said, "That won't help. Reuben's never going to get his buddies at the station to hear it. Not about the guy who used to buy him drinks at Tujague's."

"If you can't make Reuben do something about it, you should fire him. Hire someone who understands who's giving the orders."

She made a sound of disbelief. "Fat chance I'd ever find anyone half as qualified who's willing to work for what I pay him."

Marcus stopped in his tracks and stared a question at her. "If he's any good, why does he work so cheap?"

She shrugged, explaining, "He's got his police retirement, for one thing. And he was a good friend of my dad's, back before he died and my mother left town with my sister and me."

Marcus opened the car door for her, his manners and the old-fashioned cut of his clothing reminding her once more how she'd described him to Detective Robinson. *He might have stepped out of the Renaissance, or a pirate movie.*

Or maybe he had been plucked from her own dreams, a drop-dead gorgeous fantasy she didn't dare embrace.

She slid inside the car and waited to speak until he pulled into traffic. "I'll take your advice. Talk to Reuben *and* the detectives. If they won't listen, I'll find some cop who will. At least Natalie spotted Paine getting in my face before he took off. She might not have heard the words, but she's a trained actress. She knows body language when she sees it."

So did Caitlyn, and Marcus's spoke volumes as he drove back to the Quarter. Frustration, anger, longing—all were written in his clenched hands, the tension in his shoulders, the aggressively stiff line of his back and his refusal to meet her eyes.

Still not looking at her, he parked a few streets

over from the mansion on Esplanade. "I don't want Reuben to get a look at the car."

"I can walk from here," she said, though in this neighborhood, she shouldn't. Particularly not with nightfall nipping at dusk's heels.

"Not without me right beside you."

He locked the car but once again brought his camera with him.

They said little as they walked, with Caitlyn stopping and splaying her hand across his strong shoulder to help her balance as she dumped a nonexistent pebble from her sandal.

Too soon, the old white mansion came into view, its columns and its verandas and its towering live oak tree all unwelcome sights.

"Thank you for the dinner," she said, her voice softer than the breath of evening that stirred the leaves of a magnolia. "And I wanted to tell you, I'm really…"

What good would it do to tell him that she would miss him? To say that part of her wished she could climb into his car and disappear with him forever?

She still had no idea what he was fleeing, or if Marcus Le Carpentier was really his name. Besides, it was nothing but a fantasy, the work of stress and hormones, to think she could leave behind her responsibilities to Jacinth and their legacy.

"I just wanted to say I'm sorry." Her words came out clipped and abrupt, a shield to hide her grief. "Sorry I broke your camera."

"I'm not." Marcus's voice went rough. "Because if you hadn't, I never would have met you, and we never would've... I know it hasn't been much, but..."

Unable to finish, he made a move to open the mansion's front gate as they reached it. She grasped his hand, meaning to warn him that the hinges squeaked and might bring Reuben running.

Before she got the words out, her gaze snagged on a shape that shouldn't be there. A shape that made no sense in the context of the flowering lantana and half-hidden by the tree trunk as it was.

Peering into the dim light, she leaned forward, studying the slender, pale form lying on the grass. A graceful white leg that narrowed to an ankle, then flattened to a bare foot.

The toenails had been painted black, Caitlyn realized in the split second before a scream tore from her.

Then they rushed into the yard and saw the naked girl behind the tree trunk, saw the cheap blond wig that she was wearing...

And the cold glass eyes of staring, lifeless green.

AT THE SOUND OF CAITLYN'S SHRIEK, Marcus saw Reuben come boiling out of the house. The retired cop seemed not to see the crumpled figure with the thin bruised line around her pale neck but ran straight for Marcus himself, as he held Caitlyn, turning her physically from a sight he wished he could erase from both their minds.

"You son of a bitch, let her go!" Reuben shouted, snatching his gun from a shoulder holster and pointing it straight at them.

Seeing it, Caitlyn cried out, interposing her body between the two men and holding up a shaking hand. "No—no, Reuben. We just got home and—I—I saw *her*. Right here. Is she— Please tell me she's not dead."

Jaw dropping as he spotted the battered body, Reuben swore and dove to his knees to check the girl's wrist for a pulse.

Certain that she *was* dead—she had to be, with that chalk-pale flesh and her blue lips—Marcus pulled Caitlyn even closer.

But she pushed him away and whispered, "Go now. Hurry," worry for him burning like a fever in her eyes.

He hesitated, torn between the need to be there protecting her and older loyalties.

Then she shook her head and silently mouthed a single word. *Please*.

"I'm sorry," he whispered to her before rushing out the gate and sprinting for the car.

He hated himself for it. For leaving Caitlyn at the precise moment she most needed his support.

And he hated Theo, too, cursed the burden of the brother who had left him with no choice except to run. Who left him almost hoping Reuben would end this with a bullet. Would put a stop to all the running, all the lying—starting with the night of his own fiancée's murder.

As he cut between two houses, the memories nearly overwhelmed him: Samantha smiling, laughing. Lying dead in her bed with the house in flames around them.

Lying naked, her throat bruised not unlike the girl he'd just seen. Except that, in Samantha's case, he knew exactly who had killed her.

You did, his conscience whispered. *It was your fault, plain and simple. Your fault for bringing her into your life and letting her be swallowed by the chaos.*

It was no wonder that Samantha's father, Isaiah's violence-prone ex-son-in-law, had sworn to kill Marcus. No wonder that he still would, even if the full truth were discovered.

Marcus emerged onto a sidewalk and spotted his Chevy parked a halfblock ahead. With a final burst of speed, he reached it, despite the hardening concrete of his anger weighing down his every step.

Chapter Nine

"Her name was Bree," Detective Davis said the following day in the interview room he and his partner had borrowed to update Caitlyn on the case.

Or at least they'd claimed it was an update. Caitlyn wasn't so sure.

"Short for Brianna," Lorna Robinson added. "Brianna Foster, a sixteen-year-old runaway reported missing up in Memphis."

Caitlyn crossed her arms over her stomach. "She was just a kid."

The balding Davis shrugged.

"A street kid and a corner whore—I mean a *prostitute,* excuse me," he added, responding to his partner's sharp look. "Which made her an easy grab."

"Is that supposed to make me feel better?" Caitlyn asked him. "Whoever's doing this is clearly focused on me. Killing these poor girls just to terrify me."

With a jingle of her many bracelets, Lorna Robinson placed a rich brown hand over Caitlyn's. "He's killing because he's evil, twisted—"

"Or 'disturbed 'cause of bad toilet trainin',' if you listen to the damned defense attorneys." Davis's oddly pointed teeth made his smile appear feral.

Combined with the long chin, he reminded Caitlyn of a talking fox… or perhaps a *rougaroux*. But she conceded that her opinion was colored by his friendship with Josiah Paine—and his phone call to Reuben suggesting her involvement.

"He does it because he likes terrifying women," Detective Robinson insisted. "Why he's settled on you is anybody's guess. Maybe he saw you on a brochure or the net, or giving one of your tours, and you reminded him of the object of his obsession from back in the eighties, when he killed those prostitutes."

"Or maybe he's a copycat—an admirer of the previous killer's work," Davis suggested. "Some of those crazies like to study old-school serials the way some kids study baseball cards. Maybe we've got ourselves a young guy smart enough to take his lessons from the one who got away.

"Which brings us to your friend, Marcus Le Carpentier," Davis went on, studying her with a look of frank appraisal.

Caitlyn tried to protest, but surprise and fear

struck her mute. Surprise that they had somehow learned his full name, since she hadn't shared it, and raw terror that maybe they had found something to connect Marcus to the two murders whose discovery he had *just so happened,* as Reuben had repeatedly pointed out, to be present to witness.

Her instincts couldn't have led her so very far wrong...could they?

Detective Robinson explained, "Too much street crime scares off tourists, so we've got video surveillance cameras scattered all over the Quarter. We ended up with a great shot of him on one of them, then plugged the first name 'Marcus' into the federal database and ran it against suspects in cases involving violence against women."

Unshed tears stung Caitlyn's eyes, and her ears filled with a rushing sound. The detective's mouth moved, but her brain couldn't make sense of his words, not until Robinson cocked an eyebrow and asked, "Are you getting any of this, Miss Villaré?"

Caitlyn shook her head, only wanting it to end so she could go home.

Detective Davis leaned forward, enunciating slowly and loudly, as if he were speaking to a foreigner. "What my partner's telling you is that Marcus Le Carpentier's a wanted man. For arson of a residence—his fiancée's apartment—to cover up her murder. According to our information, the cops in Pennsylvania say he choked her with his bare hands."

Garish images splashed through Caitlyn's mind: the necks of the dead women, with their thin, dark lines of bruising. Clapping a palm against her mouth, she scrambled to her feet so quickly, her chair tipped. Its metal back cracked like a thunderclap as it bounced off the floor.

"For four years, he's been running," Davis added. "Leaving God knows how many dead girls around the country."

Caitlyn glared at him. "I can't believe that. I won't." This ugly *rougaroux* was lying, just to rile her up.

Though Davis sneered, what looked like sympathy filled Lorna Robinson's light hazel eyes. "Women have been saying that about the men they love since the dawn of time. I've said it myself about both of my ex-husbands, even when I knew in my heart they were lyin' cheaters."

"I'm not in love with Marcus Le Carpentier." Caitlyn's stomachache intensified with her denial. "But what you're saying, it doesn't make sense. If he's from Pennsylvania, how can you expect anyone to believe he'd know about those old murders in New Orleans?"

"N'awlins is his hometown." Sadness tinged Detective Robinson's voice.

Davis checked a notepad and gloated, "The family lived here 'til the early nineties. Stroke got the mother real young. Then the dad took the kids and headed back East for a job."

"You said he used his hands to—to strangle his fiancée." Caitlyn shook her head, desperately grasping at the thinnest of straws. "But the two victims I found— those lines on their necks looked like… I can't think what you'd call them, but—"

"Ligature marks—like someone used a strap or rope, you mean?" Davis shrugged. "So his signature's evolving, or he's modeling his crime after the killings he heard about as a kid."

Caitlyn shook her head. "How could he possibly have dumped the body in my front yard, where anyone could have seen it, when he was with me for at least two hours before I found it?"

"Killers like this," Davis said, "have been known to team up with an accomplice. And Bree Foster had been dead for at least twelve hours before she was found."

"I don't believe it," Caitlyn repeated.

Lorna Robinson stood to look her directly in the eye and challenged, "Don't you, Caitlyn?"

Though the two detectives badgered her for a few more minutes before Caitlyn finally decided she'd had enough and walked out, that was the one question that stuck with her, echoing in her head like an unwanted snatch of song.

And crashing against memories of Reuben calling her naive, and her sister's constant warnings that if she weren't more careful, she was sure to end up hurt.

Right again, Jacinth, Caitlyn thought. *As always.*

AROUND DUSK THE NEXT EVENING, Marcus swapped the Chevy for a beat-up Dodge truck with a faded paint job, and a host of dings and dents that contrasted with a shiny new rear bumper. Where he was heading, looks didn't count for much. It was the Ram's strong engine and off-road capability that mattered.

With his photo series finished and the images safely in Isaiah's hands, Marcus knew he should make the call he had been dreading and begin his long journey to the border. Instead, he parked the pickup and took one last walk along the riverfront. He kept to himself, avoiding the couples chattering and laughing as they hurried toward a brilliantly lit paddle wheeler for a dinner cruise.

Sitting on an empty bench to down the shrimp po'boy sandwich he had picked up, he watched the Mississippi's muddy waters flowing toward the Gulf. Flowing home, as every river must. As he himself had finally done, though in the end it had brought him no peace, only the painful memory of the single meal he'd shared with a woman who had made him long for things he'd given up the right to. Who had stirred the ashes of hope he'd believed too cold to rekindle.

Now it burned in his gut, the knowledge that Caitlyn Villaré existed. That he could never claim her. Couldn't even stay here to be certain she was safe.

Appetite gone, he pitched the rest of the sandwich into a trashcan, then started walking along the river to brace himself for the bad news he was about to deliver.

His sister answered on the third ring, sounding rushed and harried, as she often did when he called.

"How's Theo?" Marcus began, as *he* always did.

"About the same," Stacey said. "Except the facility's raising the rates again. Another five hundred a month, starting in August. Sorry to break the bad news to you."

"I'm the one who's sorry," Marcus told her. "Sorry I can't help you with the day-to-day."

"Would you mind if we cut this short? I have to pick up a prescription the doctor called in for Hailey. If you could just be sure to transfer the extra money—"

"Is she okay?" Marcus tried to picture the niece

he'd never seen, a nearly four-year-old girl her mother had described as a brown-eyed munchkin in long pigtails. It hurt like hell to think that she would grow up with no knowledge of her uncle. Of either uncle, since Stacey wasn't crazy enough to allow her daughter anywhere near Theo.

"She'll be fine. She just picked up some stomach bug at preschool, and *of course* she turned out to be allergic to the first medicine the doctor prescribed. The one I'll have to throw away now, forget about the sky-high co-pay."

Marcus heard the frustration in her words. As a single mom and overworked nurse's aide, Stacey had her hands full and then some.

"Before you go, I have to tell you—" He gripped the handrail tightly, sucked in a breath tasting of the muddy river bottom and conceded failure. "The money's running out. Not today or next week, but very soon—and permanently. You'll have to find another place—maybe a state hospital—for him."

She gave a strangled cry. "No, Marcus. We can't do that to him. *You* can't."

"I'm sorry. But Isaiah's dying." It hurt like hell to say the words aloud. "He says there isn't much time."

"Sell your pictures on your own, then. They're wonderful. Amazing. Every bit as good as that half-blind old—"

"Without his name, they're worth nothing," Marcus interrupted, not wanting to hear her run down the man who had done so much for him. For all of them. "I don't even have a studio, or an agent of my own, let alone the kind of fame that—"

"I know you'll think of something. You always do."

The absolute faith in his younger sister's voice made him wince. Still, he found himself promising, "You can believe I'll do everything in my power, take on any kind of work. But, Stace? You do know Theo's not getting any better? No matter what we do, he'll never be the boy we—"

"We can't give up now," she pleaded. "*You* can't. I wasn't going to tell you 'til it happened, but Theo's neurologist's been telling me the FDA's almost ready to approve a new medication. There's no guarantee, of course, but the blind studies are so promising. In Europe, it's done wonders, and in Mexico they've seen a huge improvement in cognition and a strong reduction in antisocial behavior."

"This whole situation isn't right. It never has been." Marcus thought about Isaiah, dying alone, about Caitlyn, in danger from a murderous stalker. About the suffering of his fiancée's grieving parents, the couple who believed their only daughter's killer still roamed free. "I'm not helping anyone like this. You're struggling, and I'm miserable, always waiting for the other shoe to drop."

"It could really work," Stacey pleaded. "We could get him back. Remember, Marcus? Do you remember the way he was, how we all were, before it happened?"

Marcus wanted to say no, wanted to deny the memory of the curly-haired prankster of the family, the laughing boy who'd never known what it was like to have a living mother, who joked his way around their hard-drinking father's ever-changing moods and made the task of helping to raise him a pure pleasure. Who had made them all laugh until the day he had plowed into a maple tree during a forbidden ride on his best friend's dirt bike.

With no helmet to protect his skull, the eight-year-old boy's world had instantly, irreparably shattered, sending out fault lines that splintered his remaining family and very quickly drove their father to his grave.

"How can we quit now," asked Stacey, her voice breaking, "after everything we've gone through? How can we give up when we're so close?"

Marcus might be able to scatter a crowd of angry bikers, but he had no defense against his sister's tears or the guilt he felt at leaving her to handle the details of Theo's treatment all on her own.

"If he goes to one of those horrible state places," she added, "he won't have any shot at all at cutting-edge therapy, just the drugs they use to keep the inmates quiet."

"I'll work on it," he said. "Try to figure out a way."

"That's all I've ever asked," she assured him, the way she assured him every time he wondered aloud about the rightness of what they were doing. "For Theo, Marcus. For our family. It's what our parents would expect, what I know you'll find some way to pull off."

As he returned to the beat-up blue pickup and started driving, he told himself again and again that he had no choice. That because he was a wanted man, ripping off art buyers had become a necessity, not a choice—a necessity that bound him to a loner's lifestyle.

An image of Caitlyn smiling across the table from him, closing her eyes as she enjoyed her last spoonful of crème brûlée, danced through his mind. But maybe he'd thought of her simply because the colorfully painted, shamelessly touristy murals he was passing marked the office of New Orleans After Dark Guided Tours. In its small lot, a flabby man in a loudly flowered shirt—Paine himself—was climbing out of the sole car present, a gleaming black Lincoln parked beneath a security light.

Leaning over his steering wheel, Marcus noted the garish collection of bumper stickers, promoting both the Saints and Paine's own business.

Purposefully, Marcus swung into the small lot, blocking the sleek car's easy exit. Though Marcus had warned himself over and over that he couldn't risk any more involvement, what would it hurt to take out a few of his frustrations on the bully who had frightened Caitlyn with his threats yesterday?

Before he could talk himself out of it, he was out of the truck, slamming the door and stalking toward Paine, who blanched but held his ground.

"Hey there, friend." As soothingly as he spoke, Paine's eyes looked tense, squinting from within the folds of fat that framed them. "You come to pick up a brochure? Or maybe an employment application?"

When Marcus didn't answer, Paine produced a handkerchief and mopped beads of perspiration from his forehead. His gaze shifted for a moment to the open door of his car, as if he were thinking of taking refuge there.

"What can I do for you, sir?" He tried again. "You got a problem? Business issue? Did a couple of my guys come 'n' see you about a loan, maybe?"

Marcus wasn't shocked at this evidence that Paine had his greasy fingers in another business, too. An illegal business like loan sharking could potentially earn far greater profits than the legitimate tour company Paine might well be using as no more than a front.

Marcus moved in even closer, and the shorter, heavier man crabbed backward, attempting to fold himself into the driver's seat.

"Get out," Marcus told him. "Get out now and I won't hurt you."

"I can be flexible with my terms," Paine bleated. "Quite reasonable. You need some more time? Payments lowered?"

"Up." Marcus gestured, waiting patiently for the fat man to rise from the car.

It was hard for him, what with that stomach, but after a moment he stood in front of Marcus. As he did, he underwent a visible transformation, his jaw tightening and his face reddening, an animal-like fury burning in his eyes.

Paine was clearly humiliated, Marcus realized, something a man known for his temper didn't suffer lightly.

"Just tell me. Tell me what you want," Paine ground out.

"I want you to stay miles away from Caitlyn Villaré," Marcus warned him. "Don't go near her. Don't call her. Don't stir up any trouble for her."

"So you're sleeping with her, are you?" Paine's snort was dismissive. "You'd hardly be the first. That Villaré girl's a tramp just like her mother. Hardly worth the—"

Marcus slammed Paine backward, into the open doorframe, where he held the man pinned, his muddy brown eyes popping wider.

"Do I have your full attention now?" Marcus seared him with a hard stare, until Paine nodded quickly, his sneer turning to a look of terror. "You're done insulting Caitlyn. You're finished threatening her. And if you even think of doing worse, I'll be back. Understand that? I'll be back when you least expect it, maybe when you're sleeping."

Another rapid-fire nod.

"And I absolutely *will* destroy you." Marcus let his gaze bore into terrified eyes. Let Paine think about what he was saying and feel the truth of his vow.

Marcus wished to God it were true, that he could stick around to enforce his threats against this coward. But he had nothing to hold over the maggot, nothing except whatever fear he might instill, for however long it lasted.

Beyond that…

Disgusted by the uselessness of his own actions, the bleakness of the wasteland that opened up before him with his violence, Marcus let go of

Paine's shirt and shoved the man away. "Go and sin no more."

As he turned to leave, he wasn't certain whether he had meant the quote for Josiah Paine or himself.

He was still pondering the question when he heard a sound behind him. A metallic noise that came an instant before Paine opened fire.

Chapter Ten

With Reuben away on a brief trip to pick up his mail and check on his house, Caitlyn set up a box fan in the attic, but although the sun had gone down, the stifling breeze did little except to stir the dust.

She sneezed and blew her nose, then started digging through the boxes she and Jacinth had spotted not long after their move. At the time, they hadn't paid much attention to the single carton marked with their mother's name. To the sisters, their grandmother Marie had been the mystery, not the familiar mom who had moved them back to her Ohio hometown and raised the two of them with loving care.

But Max Lafitte's cruel comments, his insistence that her mother was a tease and her father quick with his fists, had gotten Caitlyn wondering. Was there more to her mom—a mother Caitlyn never once remembered going on dates, much less flirting shamelessly—than she had ever guessed?

A wave of guilt struck at her doubt, sweeping her against a solid wall of grief. She struggled not to think of her mother's last days, before swift-moving cancer took her, and not to feel disloyal for questioning a past that the former Sophie Sinclair had more than earned the right to leave behind.

Caitlyn's fingers smeared the dust atop the box, revealing only her mother's first name, in slashing, angry-looking letters. Had her grandmother packed up the last unwelcome reminders of her murdered son's bride? What had happened to cause such bitterness between the two that Caitlyn's mother forever after refused to speak of the place she'd once called home?

After switching off the fan, she carried the box down two flights of stairs and into the kitchen, the one room where the dying AC had made a respectable last stand. At the breakfast table, she made short work of the dust and used a knife to slit the yellowed packing tape.

She had only pried up the first flap when she heard the screech of tires in the street out front.

Fear pinching inside her, she glanced reflexively at the countertop, where Reuben had insisted on leaving a loaded pistol in case she needed it in his absence, though Caitlyn had sworn she would never touch the thing. Ignoring it in spite of her fear, she hurried into the formal living room and cautiously peered past the heavy curtain covering one of a pair of impressively tall windows.

Directly in front of the house, an older pickup truck had pulled into the spill of light beneath an antique-style street lamp. Though she had never seen the vehicle before, she gasped with the shock of recognition as Marcus struggled out, the shoulder of his white shirt gleaming black.

Not truly black, she knew instinctively. If she had a light to shine on it, it would glow with the deep red of fresh blood.

She was halfway to the front door before caution kicked in. What if the blood she'd spotted wasn't his? What if he had killed again, as he was accused of doing in Pennsylvania? As the detectives and Reuben believed he might have done here, too?

Indecision froze her in place, and she could almost hear Reuben's gravelly voice ordering, *Call 9-1-1.*

From out front, she heard the gate creak, and her own instincts shouted loudly, *It's Marcus, and he's hurt. Get out there and help him.*

With her stomach in knots, she ran back to the kitchen, her hand reaching toward the gun that lay there gleaming coolly, its black metal reassurance crafted for only one purpose: shooting down a human being. But as squeamishness gave way to self-preservation, she picked it up and held it out before her, hating its cold touch, yet feeling its seductive power flowing through her.

She reached the front door just before his knocking started, loud and urgent. As she had before, she opened it but kept the chain in place and the pistol out of sight.

This close, she smelled the blood on his shirt and saw that the wound was on his upper arm rather than his shoulder. Pain had leached the color from his handsome face, streaking it with perspiration.

"Oh, Marcus. I'm calling you an ambulance."

"No—no police, no ambulance." His hand trembled as he reached toward her. "Just let me inside, please. I waited 'til Reuben left, but I really need some bandages or clean towels. I'll be okay if I can stop the bleeding."

Her hand shot to the chain, where she hesitated as she looked into his desperate eyes. Hesitated as the meaning of his words slammed through her. He had waited—despite the condition he was in—for Reuben to leave her all alone. ...

And he was on the run for burning down his fiancée's home to hide her murder.

Could he have feigned this wound, even gone so far as to hurt himself, to get her to let her guard down? She imagined the mansion in flames, her own body lying inside it.

Heartbeat drumming in her ears, she forced herself to tell him, "I'm sorry, Marcus, but I'm either calling 9-1-1 or you're going to have to leave now. And if that's your choice, don't bother coming back."

"Caitlyn, listen to me. It was Josiah Paine who did this."

Why would Paine…? She let go of the thought, shaking her head. "I know who you are, Marcus. I know what you did in Pennsylvania. So which is it? Do I make the call now and get help for you? Or are you leaving—"

"I swear, I never…" Behind his eyes, a wall came up, and he turned to stagger away. "You're right. I should leave now. Better for both of us this way."

The pain in his voice, the bitter disappointment, was nearly her undoing. Closing the door as he walked away, she leaned against it, pressing a hand against her throbbing temples.

And then she heard the crash a minute later.

Acting on pure instinct, she unchained the door and ran outside, to where Marcus's pickup had knocked down a section of the iron fence and come to rest between the massive live oak and the smaller magnolia in the front yard. Though the truck didn't appear badly damaged, he was slumped over the steering wheel, apparently unconscious.

"Marcus!" she cried as she rushed nearer. She looked around frantically for help, but she spotted no passersby or neighbors, and only one car, which first slowed down and then squealed away when the frightened driver, a horrified-looking young Asian woman, saw the gun in Caitlyn's hand.

Caitlyn called his name again, but Marcus didn't stir until she nudged the arm hanging limply from the open window.

He roused, barely lifting his head, and even in the dim light, she saw how colorless his lips were, how unfocused his dark eyes. "Inside, Caitlyn. Tie my hands—whatever you want. Just help me stop the bleeding."

She stood very still, feeling balanced on a knife's edge, knowing that whichever way she moved, the decision would slice her to the bone.

THE NIGHT SPINNING AROUND Marcus stank of blood and sweat, overlaid with the sweetly floral scent of a magnolia blooming nearby. When the world came to rest, he saw that Caitlyn was still staring, the anguish of uncertainty written in her green eyes.

But it was the pistol in her right hand that tormented him even more than the pain of the gunshot wound to his arm. Until now, he'd thought of her as his angel, an innocent to be protected.

More like an innocent to be corrupted by her association with him.

Because she'd learned the truth—or what she thought to be the truth—of his past, now she was terrified to trust him. Too afraid to let him come inside, even at gunpoint.

Resolve hardening her eyes, she reached out and opened the truck door, her answer written on her face.

"In the house," she said. "Quick—before anybody sees you. And don't think for a second I won't defend myself."

He staggered ahead of her, using the railing to pull himself up the front steps.

"Go ahead," she urged. "Go on in."

He continued to hesitate at the heavy wooden front door, positioned between two of the massive columns. It was the kind of entrance built to keep the likes of him out.

The hell with that, he thought, blinking away the dizziness and yanking the door open with his good arm. In the entryway, his footsteps echoed off the marble, and above his head, he caught glimpses of a chandelier, and the classical fauns and satyrs dancing in the dome above it. He noticed, too, the imperfections, the peeling paint and crumbling plaster, the rust-colored stain in

Colleen Thompson   135

the hallway ceiling and the subtle scent of mildew that hinted at a leak.

Run-down or not, had any Le Carpentier ever rested his head inside a house as grand as this one?

"You might want to grab a towel," he warned. "I'm dripping."

She returned with one in seconds and looked relieved to see him still standing where she'd left him. "Water's out in the downstairs bathroom. Can you make it upstairs?"

At his nod, she explained, "At least I'm well-stocked with plenty of antiseptic cream and bandages. Someone's forever getting bruised or scraped up trying to keep this place from falling down around our ears."

Though she sounded stressed, he heard affection in her voice, too, as well as pride in the faded grandeur of her home.

He shoved the damp hair from his eyes. "Let's just use the kitchen—I don't want to make a lot of trouble for you. I just need to explain—"

"Up the stairs, and hurry," she insisted, gesturing with the pistol.

Why was it she wanted him up there so badly? Her eyes offered no clue. He read only anxiety, probably because she wasn't used to handling a weapon. Reminding himself that made her twice as likely to squeeze off a shot from nervousness, he decided not to argue and instead did as she asked, his injured arm throbbing in protest.

Still, he felt uneasy as the steps creaked under his footsteps. He walked ahead of her, his hand gliding along the rich mahogany banister. When he spotted a small bathroom and started inside, she said, "No, not there. All the way down on the right."

They passed several huge wooden doors before he peered inside a warm and stuffy bedroom, dimmed by a pair of heavy crimson curtains on a window he realized would face the side of the house next door. Among the shadows, he made out the hulking forms of a heavy carved bed and a large dark wardrobe, and a ladies' vanity set with a mirror and a stool.

"My grandmother's suite," Caitlyn explained, ushering him inside. "The bathroom's there, to the right. You'll have everything you need."

Before he could ask a single question, the bedroom door snapped shut, leaving him alone. He heard a key rattling in the lock beneath the crystal knob. Uselessly, he tried the door and called out, "Caitlyn?"

The only answer was the rhythm of fast-receding footsteps, followed by the fainter sound of feet descending the stairs.

Had she left him trapped here so she could call

the authorities? Or maybe she was waiting for her pit bull to return.

His heart thundered, its every wild beat shooting agony through oozing flesh and perforated muscle. The pain of her betrayal, though he understood it rationally, hurt him even worse.

The thought of being locked up sent panic ripping through him. These past four years, for all their emptiness, he'd had nothing to his name except the sense that he was acting freely, making his own choices, as difficult as they were. Including the decision to come here, both for help and to warn Caitlyn that Paine was every bit as violent as she feared.

Except now she had made her *own* choice, closing the door, quite literally, on him forever. And potentially robbing him of any control over his own future—or his family's.

He rattled the knob again. With a burst of strength flooding his veins, he hurled his uninjured left shoulder several times against wood so heavy and solid, it barely creaked with the impact. Cursing in frustration, he gave up and staggered, breathing hard, into the bathroom.

There he tore open drawers and cupboards in search of the supplies she had promised. But as he dug them out, the question repeatedly echoed through his mind: Should he clean and dress the wound, or risk his neck attempting to climb out the second-story window in a bid for freedom?

And would it be worth it for the sake of the brother who had cost him everything he'd ever loved?

Chapter Eleven

By the time Caitlyn grabbed her purse to hide the gun and reached the pickup, her next-door neighbors had come over to check out the commotion. Dread knotted in her stomach, not because she didn't like the aging gay couple or wish them well in renovating their new purchase for a bed-and-breakfast, but the two men were so relentlessly friendly that any conversation could easily stretch into an hours-long chat-fest over cocktails.

Thinking quickly, she came up with a lie involving a ne'er-do-well boyfriend who'd had one too many.

"And not a word to my uncle about this, either, please," she added, mentally crossing her fingers as she referred to Reuben. "He already can't stand Stefan, and he's going to be furious about the fence."

Chuckling, the neighbors gave their word and even helped her back the truck out of her front yard and hide it in the mansion's dilapidated carriage house.

"Now that we're coconspirators, you'll have to come and visit us more often." The tanned, still-handsome Ernest winked, the ice cubes clinking in the highball glass he'd brought out with him.

"If I pull this off, the drinks are on me," she promised, though she'd never really taken to the taste of alcohol.

The moment they disappeared from view, she readjusted the purse on her shoulder and made a beeline for the back door, so she could check on Marcus. Finding it locked, she cursed, then used the driveway to walk around to the front…

Where she found Reuben standing outside his still-running car and studying the damaged fence.

Zeroing in on her, he glared and asked, "What the hell good are those deadbolts if you unlock them and start walking around outside?"

Her anxiety spiked, seeing him back so soon. If he discovered Marcus in the house, all hell was bound to break loose. How could she keep the two of them apart? "I heard the crash, but by the time I looked out the window, the car was speeding off, so I came to check the damage."

He turned on her, clearly furious. "I asked you to stay inside, not to even answer the door. Two women killed, one of them left for you right on this lawn, and you still don't listen to one damned thing I tell you. Are you stupid, crazy or just plain suicidal?"

"Last I checked, *you* worked for *me*." Caitlyn narrowed her eyes, but try as she might to look and sound tough, her heart sagged at the pain that flared in the huge man's eyes. Still, she went on hurting the man who loved her and kept her safe—all for the sake of a virtual stranger she had no business trusting. "You might've been my dad's friend, but let's get one thing straight. You're not my father. You're an employee. And as of right this minute, you are off the clock."

"Caitlyn, Caitlyn, *chère*. I know I get outta line sometimes. I'm sorry. But you can't afford to do this, not now. It's not safe."

"Go home, Reuben. Go, and…" Her voice gentled. "And I'll call you in the morning, okay? I just need a little time to cool off."

"I'm not leavin' you on your own. I'll sit out front in the freakin' car if that's what it takes."

Caitlyn huffed out an exasperated sigh, then nearly choked at the sight of the dark side window of her grandmother's room, with its curtains fluttering in the breeze. Had Marcus opened the window to cool the stifling room, or was he attempting to escape? Her throat tightened, and her eyes stung. Weak as he was, he would fall for certain, maybe to his death.

Turning her attention to Reuben, she offered

him a peek at the gun inside her bag. "See, I have the gun you gave me right here. I listened to you, and I'm carrying it wherever I go.

"Besides," she added, "we both know you can't keep sleeping on that awful sofa forever. I know it's killing your back. You're hunched over like an old man."

She had offered him an upstairs bedroom, but he'd refused, so he could better listen for any attempted ground-floor break-in.

"That's all you see here? An old man?" Anger flashed through his expression, and pride pushed out his chest. "I can sleep there 'til this lunatic who's stalking you is in jail. Or buried, if I've got anything to say about it."

She shook her head. "I'm going straight inside, locking the front deadbolt, and double-checking all the other doors and windows. Then you're going home until tomorrow morning."

"You'll keep the phone with you?"

She nodded. "I've got you on my speed dial."

"You have any trouble, you call 9-1-1 first, then me, and if you need to, you shoot that scum-sucking killer full of holes."

"As Swiss cheese, Reuben. Promise."

At the door, she waved to show him she was fine, then closed it behind her and quickly turned the deadbolt. She tried to count to ten, to check to see if he would really drive away. But with her fear for Marcus building, she made it only to three before she turned and sprinted up the stairs, her heart nearly bursting with her panic.

Reaching her grandmother's room, she fumbled for the key and shouted, "Marcus, are you all right? Are you in there?"

Please, God, let him be inside. Let him still be breathing.

Perspiration beading her flesh, she twisted the key inside the lock and prayed he wasn't playing possum inside, setting her up to jump her. With Reuben's warnings ringing in her ears, she took out the gun and turned the knob before using her foot to push the door.

It swung open in a smooth arc before it banged against the wall behind it. Ahead of her, shadows twisted, cast by the fluttering curtains. But nothing else inside moved, and the only light spilled from the half-closed bathroom doorway.

"Marcus?" *Was he gone already?* "Marcus, are you in there?"

Her gaze swept over the furnishings as she wondered whether he could be hiding somewhere, waiting for her to be foolish enough to step inside. But it was the memory of him passed out inside the truck and the worry that she'd made a foolish mistake in not calling the paramedics that had her edging inside. One step, two…and then she cried out, spotting his bloodstained hand in the bathroom doorway.

"SHH, DON'T TRY TO TALK. Just lift your head and have some water."

Marcus blinked in the light, then squinted to see Caitlyn hovering above him, her beautiful face lined with worry.

His head felt weighted to the floor by anchors, but he managed to raise it enough to drink. Blissfully cold, the water traced a soothing path from throat to stomach, its taste so welcome that he groaned.

"Here, let's sit you up," Caitlyn said. "Lean your back against the cabinet."

With her help he succeeded, grimacing when he forgot himself and tried to push himself up off the tile, an act that sent pain shooting through his right arm.

"Take these." She pushed several pills toward his mouth, her fingertip lingering a bare moment against his lips.

He took them without protest and swallowed them with more water.

"Tylenol," she explained. "And a couple of antibiotics I had from a while back."

He nodded, though his head pounded with the movement. And then he must have dozed.

When he woke again, he was still slumped

against the cabinet. Once he shrugged off the towel she'd thrown over him, he saw that his arm had been neatly bandaged. She must have cleaned up what he'd discovered to be a through-and-through wound.

Head spinning, he cursed every action movie hero he had ever seen wincing after a "mere flesh wound" and returning to the fray. Instead, he lay here, feeling bulldozed, while Caitlyn...

He smiled, recalling how close he had come to trying his luck with the sheer drop beneath the window when he'd realized she was outside hiding his truck. Covering his presence instead of calling the police.

Surely that must mean he still had a chance to explain. To be certain she was safe before he turned his back on New Orleans—on her—forever.

"Caitlyn?" In the instant it took for her name to reverberate in the small bathroom, he dared to hope that she would answer. That his angel would listen to his explanation, would even tell him she understood his motives.

But Caitlyn *didn't* answer, and by the time he pulled himself upright and staggered to the bedroom door, he found it locked again, so firmly that he wondered if she would ever trust him again.

THE DOLLS HAD WHISPERED warnings, telling him that she wouldn't be true, that she loved another.

Even after he had brought his offerings, his tributes to her beauty, she locked herself inside her crumbling castle of a dollhouse. But she didn't stay by herself, or hadn't for more than a few minutes.

Even when she emerged, so deliciously alone, others watched out for her. Eyes that peeked through white lace curtains. Hands that twitched toward phones in their eagerness to call the law down on his head.

But for all their precautions, the time was creeping steadily, inexorably nearer. The time— this very night, he swore, as his heating blood pounded throughout his aching body—when he would take her, killing anyone who stood in his way....

Especially the thieving bastard who sought to steal his doll bride. The doll bride who would reign over her silent legion of attendants.

She would be silenced, too, once he claimed his rights as her groom. He would see to it. He would have to....

For as hard of hearing as his mother now was, she never had *been able to abide the sound of screams.*

Chapter Twelve

When was it, Caitlyn wondered, that she had passed the point of no return? Had it been when she had lied for Marcus, then hidden a pickup she had never seen before? Or had it happened when she'd invited him inside? Or perhaps her loss of sanity had been preordained from the very start, from the moment she had knocked the camera out of his hands, an accident that had shattered not only his lens but her future?

Whenever it had happened, things had gone too far. She couldn't just keep a man who'd been shot—a possible murderer, for God's sake— either a prisoner or a pet inside her house.

She couldn't afford to be this crazy. She had to get him out. Twice she reached for the phone, first meaning to call Reuben, and then the number Detective Robinson had given her. But each time she ended up folding her arms over her roiling stomach and pacing the confines of her kitchen.

I could let Marcus go...give him back his keys and escort him out at gunpoint.

But the idea of freeing a man wanted for a woman's murder left her just as unsettled as the thought of keeping him there. And if she refused to listen to him, how would she ever find out what had really happened between him and Paine? Presuming that anything that Marcus told her could be trusted...

Distracted by her quandary, she missed Sinister's beeline for her ankles and was deaf to his cries for a belated dinner. Feet tangling around the Persian, Caitlyn yelped and tried to catch herself on the kitchen table. Her hand struck the carton of her mother's things and overturned the box, dumping it onto the floor before she recovered her balance.

"Stupid hairball," she said, as Sin sped off to safety. Looking at the mess, she felt like sentencing the little demon to dry kibble for a month.

Kneeling beside the box, she began picking up an odd assortment: a stuffed lamb—perhaps Jacinth's—a baby's rattle that might have belonged to either one of them, a few dried-out old lipsticks, and a pretty hairbrush, its back carved with a fleur-de-lis inlaid with mother-of-pearl.

Then she came upon the photos. Pictures of her family—her whole family—the first Caitlyn had ever seen. Besides the tiny blond-fuzzed infant that must have been her, she recognized her sister, an adorable, round-cheeked toddler, and their dad, a strapping, handsome man with the same dark hair and eyes as Jacinth.

But what took her breath away was the fact that in every photo she found, her mother's face had been blacked out, the ballpoint pen digging so deep that in many cases holes had been left in the photos. Staring at the damage, Caitlyn felt sick. What could her gentle, hardworking mom possibly have done to provoke such hatred?

Desperate for a clue, she looked at what remained of her mother's image. Here and there, she caught a glimpse of blond hair, longer than the short and easy cuts Caitlyn recalled her mother favoring. She was slimmer, too, her curves set off by colorful blouses and skirts that nearly reached the knee. Appealing, tasteful outfits, and Caitlyn saw nothing in them to reinforce Max Lafitte's cruel words.

"She was young and pretty, that's all," she told Sinister as he sauntered back into the kitchen. "Young and pretty and happy with my father. And you were jealous of them, Max. You were jealous of what they had."

Caitlyn said the words aloud, needing to believe them, and because Sin didn't argue, she forgot her grudge and fed him, willing herself to forget the man lying in her grandmother's suite upstairs.

Afterward she picked up the last of the box's scattered contents, including a shabby-looking copy of the classic children's book *Goodnight Moon.* When a worn cover separated, one last snapshot slipped out....

Despite its faded colors, Caitlyn gasped to see it, half convinced that she was looking at a picture of herself....

Of herself and not the mother who had looked so much like her in her youth that if she were here now, they might have been mistaken for twins.

LIKE A CAGED TIGER, Marcus paced the cramped confines of his two-room prison.

"Better get used to it," he mumbled, thinking that wherever the state of Pennsylvania sent him after he was extradited, his cell would undoubtedly be far smaller and much more Spartan. Worse yet, he would never be alone in prison, never again have the freedom to relax his guard for a moment.

At that moment, though, he would have given everything he owned for company, as long as it was Caitlyn and he could see and speak to—and touch, some desperately delusional corner of his brain prayed—her. Did she intend to leave him locked here, injured and alone, all night?

As he walked, his arm throbbed out a painful rhythm, barely diminished by the mild painkiller he had taken. His mind, too, refused to allow him to rest as, again and again, his instincts, finely honed by years as a fugitive, warned him to find some way out of this trap before she called the police.

Once more he went to the window, this time sticking his head out to search for some means of climbing down that wouldn't involve a broken leg or, worse, his neck. But rather than a way out, a movement quickly caught his eye. A person hidden in the shadows beneath the live oak tree, inside the wrought-iron fence surrounding the mansion's front yard.

Marcus's mind flashed to the girl's nude body that had been so recently left there. Had the killer come back with yet another hideous "present" for Caitlyn to find? Or, this time, did he mean to have the real focus of his obsession rather than a stand-in?

Rushing to the bedroom door, Marcus started hammering and rattling the locked knob. "Caitlyn, open up! There's someone hiding out front."

Whoever it was, Marcus dared to hope he might be frightened off by the noise. When Caitlyn didn't answer, he made another run at the door, but the heavy wood remained impossibly solid. He called her name again, thinking that she had to have heard the banging and the shouting.

"Get your gun!" he ordered. "I swear, some-one's outside."

The answering silence swallowed him whole, sending his adrenaline into overdrive. Could the killer have gotten in the house by this time?

He checked the window but could no longer make out the figure that had been there. Was Caitlyn failing to answer because she couldn't— not while she was being strangled by whatever her stalker had pulled tight around her neck?

With the marrow-freezing thought, Marcus stepped back, preparing to make one final run at the door.

That was when he noticed the vulnerable hinges. Hinges whose pins he could pry free, if he could only find something to use as a tool.

AFTER HEARING MARCUS BANGING, Caitlyn had been halfway upstairs when she understood that he was yelling about someone out front and urging her to get her gun.

She froze in her tracks, her legs encased in concrete. But his persistent, increasingly desper-ate shouts convinced her to check out his claim.

Pistol trembling in her hand, she turned around and crept back downstairs. Rather than flipping on the front lights as she would have liked to, she crept into the darkened living room and peered out the front window.

She stared until her eyes watered but saw nothing but darkness so impenetrable, she might have had a hood thrown over her head. Hoping for a better angle, she crept to the second window and pushed the velvet curtain to one side.

Quivering, she aimed her gaze toward the streetlight, and this time she made out several silhouettes. Most, she recognized, were from the bent boughs of the live oak, bearded here and there with moss that nodded in the night breeze, and the prison bar-like wrought iron of the gate.

Among them, she distinguished a different sort of shape, stooped and slender, a form carved of obsidian. Caitlyn squinted, pressing her face to the glass and letting the dark curtain fall behind her to block the light trickling in from the hall.

Yet she had no idea what the thing was until it broke free of the surrounding darkness and rushed directly at her, like a bat bursting from the screaming mouth of hell.

Chapter Thirteen

Shrieking, Caitlyn tried to back away but got tangled in the curtains. Frantically, she fumbled with the gun, bringing it upward just as, on the other side of the glass, no more than two feet before her, a face burst from the darkness.

A woman's face. Ashen, gaunt and wrinkled, it was lit up from below, by the flashlight she was aiming upward.

A trick! Caitlyn's rational mind shouted. A trick to frighten children while telling scary stories.

But it was horrifying nonetheless, with Eva Rill's monstrous mouth twisting, shaping curses, shouting through the glass in words so loud they vibrated the panes.

"Away with you!" she shrilled, the ancient voice crackling with power. "Leave New Orleans forever. Leave here. Leave him alone!"

From upstairs, Caitlyn heard a loud bang, a

sound she ignored as she focused on the threat before her.

"Get out of here, you lunatic. The police are on their way!" she screamed at the old woman. "Go now, or I'll shoot."

The crone dropped her chin and leveled a deadly, dark-eyed gaze at Caitlyn. "You don't fool me, little girl. You're not a killer, you're a sacrifice. A victim, pure and simple. *His* victim, if you won't go. You're running out of time."

From the folds of her black cloak, the old woman drew a pistol of her own, a long-barreled antique, a gun that looked so ancient, it might have been a stage prop.

With a cry of terror, Caitlyn dove sideways, the heavy curtain falling back in place to block both her view and Eva Rill's.

As footsteps thundered down the stairs, a loud blast, then a second, were followed by the tinkling of glass. Heart slamming against her breastbone, Caitlyn looked up from the floor where she had fallen to see twin bullet holes in the thick fabric, the streetlight dimly shining through them.

So much for the idea that the old woman's gun had been a stage prop.

"Caitlyn!" Marcus's voice echoed in the dark entryway. "Are you hurt?"

It occurred to her that she should have been frightened that he'd escaped his makeshift prison.

But her horror over having nearly been killed trumped every other worry.

"She's right outside. She tried to shoot me!"

"Did she hit you?" he asked.

Caitlyn forced her brain to slow down, to take inventory of her body. "I'm okay, I think. But she's still out there."

"Stay down," Marcus ordered.

But she was already scrambling away from the window, climbing to her feet and running toward him to throw herself into his arms. At Marcus's grunt of pain, she reflexively jerked back, recalling his injury.

Recalling her fear of him, and the reason for it.

When she moved, he caught her wrist in his good hand.

Caught her wrist and snatched away the gun.

Marcus headed toward the back of the house, searching for a way out.

"No, wait!" called Caitlyn, as she weighed the risks of following him against the threat from outside. Choosing the devil she knew, she said, "Don't go."

He turned his head, surprise flaring in his eyes, before he asked, "Just who is it I'm chasing? You said 'she.'"

"It's Eva Rill—the old woman from your photo.

But stay inside, please. She has a gun, and she'll shoot."

"I think we've established that," Marcus said dryly. Spotting a back door, off the kitchen, he unlocked the deadbolt. "Lock up after me, and turn off the downstairs lights. Then keep away from all the doors and windows."

"She could hurt you."

"She's the one who'd better worry." Taking a deep breath, he mentally pushed back the pain of his injured arm and stepped through the open door.

Outside, he waited, listening for her to do as he'd asked and get back from the door, before bending down and slipping toward the front of the house.

Navigating the deepest shadows, he stalked an enemy who might very well be lying in wait, planning to blast away at the first sign of movement. Who might very well be working in concert with the man who had brutally murdered two young women.

He crept forward, the hand holding the gun growing slick with perspiration, and all his senses straining for a shape, a sound, a scent, that didn't belong. But it was a taste that warned him—the electric bite of raw adrenaline—a bare instant before a shot splintered the darkness.

He dove behind the live oak, the same tree he

had earlier run into with his pickup. This time it proved a lifesaver, its thick trunk shielding him from the bullet that cracked against the wood.

Popping back out, he aimed the pistol in the direction of the sound. But he held his fire, hearing the clunk of a vehicle's door closing. Rushing toward it, he froze, stunned as a pair of headlights jumped onto the sidewalk and a huge black car barreled toward him.

Leaping to one side, he rolled onto one shoulder, meaning to pop back to his feet and smoothly lift the gun. But halfway up, a wave of agony washed over him, the pain of his half-forgotten injury. Blackness slashed across his vision, and by the time he recovered, he caught only a glimpse of receding taillights before they disappeared around the corner.

He cursed violently, certain the old woman had pulled off an escape with the help of her accomplice, and equally sure that by the time he retrieved his truck, he would never catch up with them.

Head spinning, he strained his attention to the breaking point but heard nothing except distant traffic. No approaching sirens, in spite of the gunfire. Perhaps no one else was home, or the neighbors might have assumed the gunfire had come from the rougher area two blocks away.

A sad statement about the area, but Marcus

took the silence as a blessing, an opportunity to head back to his pickup. To head back and head out, assuming Caitlyn had left the keys inside it. If not, he could use the hot-wiring skills he had picked up to start the engine, then put New Orleans in the rearview forever. Yet the thought of leaving Caitlyn to face this nightmare on her own wrung the breath from his lungs.

He tried to shrug off his unwillingness to leave, telling himself that what he felt was nothing but an urge to bed her, unlikely and unwise as it was. The beautiful green eyes, the blond hair, the slender curves that called his body like a beacon. Nothing but his hormones leading him to trouble.

But no matter how hard he tried, he knew damned well that he was lying. Lying to himself to think that any other woman would affect him the same way. Powerless to stop himself, he returned to knock at Caitlyn's back door.

When she didn't immediately answer, he called, "It's me! I didn't see her, but evidently she drew a bead on me."

Nervous as she was, Caitlyn must have heard the gunshot and the squeal of tires. Was she afraid to draw the old woman's attention back to herself? "She's long gone now," he assured her. "It's safe to open up."

He would swear he felt Caitlyn on the other side of the door, wavering between the man she thought she knew and the killer she'd been warned of. A man so evil, he would strangle and then burn the body of a woman he had promised to love and protect.

"If you let me back in, I can explain things," he said. "I'll tell you what happened in Pennsylvania. All of it, I swear."

"Put down the gun," she called, "and step away. Move back and put your hands up."

He should turn now, run for his life and for Theo's future. Run for another chance to set up something with his mentor and the attorney who handled Isaiah's affairs.

But Caitlyn called him to her, the way the Gulf called to the river. And like the Mississippi, he was compelled to flow toward her embrace.

"Okay." He turned a moment before squatting. "The gun's up against the door."

Moving to a safe distance, he showed his empty hands and waited. The door opened, and she grabbed the pistol, then stood pointing it his way.

"I'm sorry, Marcus," she murmured. "But you can come inside now."

Once indoors, he waited while she locked up, and then, at her bidding, walked ahead of her into the kitchen, where he sat at the counter. To his astonishment, she turned her back to him and started scooping coffee into the brew basket.

Wondering if she'd completely changed her mind about him, he asked, "You aren't worried I'll sneak up behind you?"

Blond waves swung as she shook her head. "And you're not worried I'll turn around and shoot before you make it three steps?"

"Probably not." He patted the front pocket of his jeans. "Since I ejected the magazine before I returned the gun."

She whirled around, her delicate brows raised. "No bullets?"

"No offense," he said, "but being shot once this evening was enough for me, and you seem a little on edge."

"You think?" A wry smile slanted across her strained face. "But what if that crazy old bat comes back? Or the killer?"

"By then I plan to have charmed you into letting me protect you." Marcus tried out a grin.

Caitlyn didn't return it, only turned again to take out a pair of mugs and clunk them down on the counter.

"Are you going to charm me the way you charmed your fiancée, Marcus?" she demanded. "Will you protect me the way you protected her?"

Marcus felt his face hardening like plaster, a mask to cover the violent upheaval inside him. "I thought the world of Samantha. I *loved* her."

As harshly as the words came out, he wondered

if they were true. Or had he merely wanted to love the shy and gentle Sam because she was Isaiah's granddaughter?

Pain shafted through his chest with the thought, a mix of grief and guilt.

"I would've given my life to keep her safe." Despite what it cost him to speak them, the words were cool and hard as plate glass. "You're right, though. I did fail her. I thought I could make him understand, but…"

The coffeemaker burbled, weaving the richly bitter scents of chicory and coffee around them like a net.

"You didn't…" Caitlyn shook her head. "You really didn't kill her?"

Though hope had been a stranger to him, he recognized it in her voice. Along with healthy skepticism.

"She didn't die by my hand, but she died because of me." He willed himself to hold her gaze. "And believe me, I will spend the rest of my life paying, whether it's in a prison cell or on the road. I'm in hell either way."

"What do you mean, she died because of you?"

He held her gaze. Lodged for years inside him, the truth had put down such deep roots that unearthing it felt like wrenching his beating heart from his chest.

"I have a brother, Theo…" he managed to say.

Her hand settled atop his on the counter. Her words were even softer. "Go on, Marcus. Tell me."

"He was such a great kid. A real live wire, and so funny. Everybody loved him."

Her fingers caressed his, the trust implicit in that simple touch quieting the storm.

"When he was only eight, it all changed," Marcus said. "He had an accident, brain injury..."

He thought about those first harrowing weeks in the hospital, the heartbreaking years in rehab afterward. Theo's frustrated outbursts as he struggled to relearn everyday skills, his inability to read or consider others' feelings, the shockingly violent outbursts that made a return to school impossible.

"A lot of those changes were pretty tough to handle. But we managed to keep him home. Even after our father died, my sister and I..." Grimacing, he shook his head. "We kept the promise we made that we would never dump Theo in a state institution, not even when he grew as big as a young bull and couldn't understand his own strength, let alone deal with his emotions or anyone else's."

"How have you managed?" Caitlyn asked.

"It's taken everything we both had, everything that we can think of, to keep him safe and happy—or at least as happy as he's capable of being."

Laying the gun down on the counter, she filled the mugs. "So you're saying that your brother—that he… Why would he…?"

"Hurt Samantha?" Eyes hazing, Marcus sipped the bitter coffee. Even four years later, he still couldn't say the word *kill*. "After I—when I found her, I knew—I damned well *knew*—how jealous he was of her. How could I have missed the signs that he had gotten so bad?"

Caitlyn ran her flattened palm along his back. "You couldn't have known, Marcus. How can anyone predict something so unthinkable?"

He glared at her, neither wanting nor deserving absolution. "He'd gone crazy, absolutely crazy."

"I'm sorry," she murmured.

"He thought— Theo had this insane idea Sam had replaced me with some kind of imposter," Marcus went on. "Because I was *happy* for a change, looking forward to the future. He decided the only way to get the *real* me back was to—to destroy—"

He screwed his eyelids tight, unable to bear the hideous memories playing like a slasher film behind them. Samantha's body, splayed on her bed. The hideous bruising against the chalky whiteness. His final glimpse of her lifeless face before the flames forced him back. "I couldn't believe what happened. Couldn't imagine how I'd missed the signs. I should've—should've—warned Samantha. Never should have brought her anywhere near our screwed-up family."

"You blame yourself." Caitlyn's soft voice floated nearby. "So you took the blame for him."

"He was a child—a damaged child. I *am* the one responsible," he ground out through his clamped jaws.

"You aren't. And it was wrong of you to keep the authorities in the dark. What if Theo hurts someone else?"

Marcus shook his head. "He won't. I'm seeing to it. Paying a fortune for a secure, private facility where he's well looked after. Selling the pictures I take—selling what's left of my soul—to keep that promise I made to my father before he died."

"But what about *you,* Marcus? You can't just sacrifice your own life by letting the police believe you were the one who—"

"Don't make me out to be so noble." Bitterness leached into his voice. "Don't act as if I don't deserve everything that's happened to me."

"You don't, and you could still set this straight."

"How? Witnesses saw me running out of her place. I had to collect myself before I went home, had to calm down so I could deal with Theo without killing him myself. Even if they hadn't come forward, as her fiancé, I was already the natural suspect."

"You could still explain, Marcus. Could let them talk to your sister, even Theo. Once he starts spouting all that body snatchers stuff, surely they'll have to realize—"

"The police are only part of the problem. Samantha's father is involved in some criminal... enterprises out of Atlantic City. He'll kill me if he tracks me down, even if he's doing it only to avenge my brother's crime. And the authorities would put Theo away, either in a prison or one of those places where they warehouse the criminally insane."

Shaking his head, he told her, "A place like that would kill him. The cage, the drugs to blot out the world... Even back when it happened, he was old enough and the crime was so violent that he'd more than likely end up certified as an adult and put in an adult institution."

"It might not be as bad as you think. Surely they've made strides in the way mentally ill patients are treated. You could check into it. Talk to an attorney about making this right."

"I can't!" he burst out. "I *won't*."

In her eyes, he saw the shifting shadow of emotion. Doubt, he thought, or it might have been foreboding.

Because an instant later the back door exploded

inward, and two uniformed men rushed in, shouting, "Police! Get your hands up! Both of you—right now!"

Chapter Fourteen

"Please—no guns," cried Caitlyn, her heart thumping toward her throat and her hands quivering above her head. "This—this is my house. He's a guest."

By the time she had the words out, an older black officer with serious brown eyes had already spun her around and handcuffed her wrists before frisking her briskly. Too stunned to react, she saw his partner, a younger white man built like a linebacker, slam Marcus so hard against the counter that he doubled over.

"Feet apart." The huge cop's voice boomed through the kitchen as he kicked at the inside of Marcus's shoe. "Wider!"

Marcus glared over his bloodstained shoulder, a look the officer rewarded by yanking his hands behind his back. Instead of relenting when Marcus grunted with pain, the man cuffed and searched him roughly, jerking his wallet from his jeans.

"Let him go," Caitlyn pleaded. "Can't you see he's hurt?"

The officer beside her shook his head, his lined face stern. "What we see now, Miss Villaré, is an injured man and a gun, after one of your neighbors called in a report of an intruder and shots fired."

"That's right. Someone *did* shoot him," she snapped. "And you're hurting his arm worse by—"

"Did *you* shoot him?" he asked pointedly, turning until she could finally make out *A. J. Timmons* on his nametag. "I can understand why you're on edge. We've all been briefed about the murder victims you discovered."

"No! I never fired my gun. I only grabbed it because some lunatic shot into my house from out front. You can see the bullet holes through the front window. I'll show you."

"Who was shooting? Did you see him? Could he still be in the area?"

"She's long gone, but it was Eva Rill—the same old woman who lured me to the cemetery. She was there, too, when I found the first body. When we…" Her gaze flicked to Marcus, but he kept his eyes straight ahead, his fixed expression offering no guidance.

The two officers exchanged a look before the larger man asked Marcus, "Did Ms. Villaré here catch you tryin' to break into her place? That why she blew a hole in you?"

"Hell, no," Marcus confirmed, his face gray with strain. "She didn't hurt me, and I wasn't breaking in. And she only…let me inside after I'd been hit." He paused several times and blinked, as if he were having difficulty keeping his eyes focused. "She wrapped my arm to stop the bleeding and…"

Caitlyn looked from Officer Timmons to his younger partner. "Please—he needs a doctor."

"And *we* need answers." Brows slanting downward, the white cop peered into Marcus's face. "Especially since our caller reported a *man* lurking outside. A man matching the description of a person of interest in two murders discovered by Miss Villaré here."

With that, his cold glance banked off her, leaving her chilled despite the heat.

Timmons looked up from his examination of Reuben's pistol. "This gun's not even loaded. No residue or odor from a recent firing, either."

"Do you believe me now?" Caitlyn asked him.

"Officer Holcomb and I are just gathering information," the big cop said, before sneering down at Marcus. "So who *did* shoot you, Mr.…?"

"No idea," Marcus said, not bothering to hide his own scorn.

No idea? Caitlyn stared at him as fresh doubt

arrowed through her. Was he keeping Paine's name out of this because he knew the business-man had department connections? Or because he'd killed her old boss?

Anxiety seared her stomach, and she forced herself to hold her tongue. To listen until she could process what was happening.

The big man, Holcomb, frowned at Marcus. "So was it the old lady?"

Marcus shook his head to indicate that he didn't know, his mouth a stubborn line. But his waxy pallor told Caitlyn that he was fighting pain and blood loss as much as the shock of being cornered after so many years on the run. Trapped and hurt, with no possible escape, she was willing to bet he was less worried about his personal future than his ability to keep providing for the same brother who'd destroyed it.

Despite the circumstances, she ached to go to him, to take his hand and offer comfort, to remind him of the peaceful oasis of the quiet meal they had shared, and the fragile trust that had prompted him to speak to her of secrets he'd kept bottled up for years.

Holcomb flipped open the wallet he had pulled from Marcus's back pocket. Plucking a driver's license from the plastic sleeve, he turned it in the light and scrutinized it carefully. "You have another ID somewhere?" he asked. "Maybe a *real* one this time?"

Looking back toward Holcomb, Marcus lifted his good shoulder in a shrug and jerked a nod toward Caitlyn. "Take off her cuffs, why don't you? She's no threat to anybody."

Though he was clearly struggling to look and sound in control, Caitlyn was alarmed to notice he was swaying slightly on his feet.

Looking to the officers, she said, "You have to call an ambulance before he passes out again. At least let him sit before he falls down."

"You'd like some coddling, wouldn't you?" Holcomb asked Marcus. "Like to stall us so you can sneak away again. Well, it's not happenin' on *my* watch."

Timmons shook his head at his partner. "We'll be getting him checked out before questioning. And he can sit down at the table. He's not going anywhere."

Turning away, he used the radio from his belt to call for an ambulance. Once finished, he pulled out a key and unlocked Caitlyn's handcuffs. "This man a friend of yours, then? 'Cause it's tough to imagine you'd let a stranger into your house under the circumstances, much less worry over his health."

"He was bleeding badly." Caitlyn rubbed at her freed wrists. "And I had a gun."

"You trusted your life to an unloaded weapon?" Timmons eyed her so dubiously that she had to snap her jaw shut to keep from blurting the explanation that Marcus had disarmed her and removed the magazine to insure she wouldn't shoot him.

Realizing how easily she might say something that could cause one or both of them trouble, she followed Marcus's lead and refused to answer any further questions. When Officer Holcomb turned from looming over Marcus to press her, she shook her head and told both officers, "Just let me speak to Detective Lorna Robinson. I'm only going through this once."

Better Robinson than her partner Davis, a man who drank with Josiah Paine and who had suggested she was using these murders for publicity. From the way they were behaving, Caitlyn suspected these two officers might well share Davis's opinions.

Timmons nodded. "We'll be glad to take you to the station. Detectives'll definitely want to talk to you."

Willing the ambulance to hurry, she looked again to Marcus, who was sitting with his eyes closed. "Can't you take his cuffs off? At least free his hurt arm?"

Ignoring her request, the veteran went to meet another officer, who showed up at the back door.

By the time the two of them had finished conferring, a siren heralded the arrival of the EMTs.

At last the beefy Holcomb freed Marcus's injured wrist, though he was quick to snap the unlocked cuff onto the stretcher and ogle the female EMT, a short woman with a blond ponytail and breasts that strained the buttons of her uniform shirt.

"I'll be ridin' with you." Holcomb's leer belied the wedding ring's gold flash on his finger. "For your protection, darlin'."

Glancing up from a perfunctory check of Marcus's vitals, the EMT sent the big cop a knowing smile. "I feel safer already. Think we're about ready to haul him."

"I'm coming, too," Caitlyn insisted, trying to imagine some way she might speak to Marcus privately. Some way she might ask him about what had really happened with Josiah.

And one last chance to decide whether she was being a fool, wanting so badly to believe Marcus's story, to trust in her bone-deep intuition that he had told her the truth. That he was no killer, but a devoted older brother protecting a boy he'd helped to raise. A brother with a terrible, uncontrollable affliction.

"You won't be going," Timmons said with a shake of his head. "I'll be taking you directly to the station."

Try as she might to argue, the officers stood firm. Timmons insisted that the long wait at Charity Hospital—always chaotic and over-crowded on the weekends—would "hinder the investigation."

But Caitlyn knew the man was lying. Knew, beyond the shadow of a doubt, that what both cops really wanted was to separate her from Marcus so they wouldn't have a chance to come together on a story.

And so she wouldn't try to interfere when they locked him in a cell.

THE AMBULANCE SLICED THROUGH black-silk darkness, its siren off, its red light swiftly pulsing. Inside the metal box, Marcus saw the intermittent wash of crimson through the grimy window, its flash lighting half the face of the female para-medic sitting at his side.

With Marcus's vitals strong and his condition stable, the curvy blonde turned her attention from Marcus's vitals to flirting with Officer Holcomb. The muscular cop grinned as he eyed her breasts, his muscles straining in a mating display that would have done a peacock proud.

The entire time his hand was resting all too close to the service weapon in its holster. A weapon he would undoubtedly make use of if Marcus so much as twitched the wrong way.

But what did it matter, now that the worst had finally happened? He had given away his freedom and, worse yet, his ability to provide for his family, all because of a weakness for a woman he could never have. A woman he wasn't even positive believed him.

From the look he'd seen on Caitlyn's face, she wasn't certain, either.

Soon enough, though, the detectives would convince her that he had killed before, which must mean he'd been somehow involved in the deaths of the two young women whose bodies had been left for her to find. She would turn from him in horror, fearing he had only meant to get close enough to kill her, or, failing that, to take advantage of her sexually.

But from the moment she had pointed a gun his way, Marcus had known she was far tougher than he had at first imagined, shrewder and more sensible than her sweet face and youthful innocence suggested.

She would have shot him, he had no doubt. Gentle vegetarian or not, she was tough enough to defend herself against anyone who made a move to harm her.

Rather than being furious that "anyone" included him, he smiled. Better she should distrust his story, distrust *him,* than fall victim to the stalker menacing her.

A stalker who might be in for the surprise of his life if he wasn't careful.

"What the hell're you smiling at?" Holcomb demanded. "You got a hole in your arm and a jail cell in your future." He slid a wink in the blonde's direction, and she giggled in response, a sound that assaulted Marcus's nerve endings like the *scritch* of nails across a blackboard.

Scowling, he zeroed in on the peacock. "I'm just looking to clear up a few questions."

It was little more than a bluff, since no matter how successful he was in convincing the detectives he had nothing to do with the recent murders, he was bound to be sent back to Pennsylvania to face the justice he had eluded for so long.

Holcomb ignored the sarcasm to smirk. "You holdin' out for the Easter Bunny, too?"

"Let's just say I'm holding out for the truth about those murdered girls. Heaven knows their families deserve more of it than you'll find chasing the wrong suspect."

Holcomb shrugged, his bulging shoulders nearly splitting the seams of his black shirt. "Maybe so, but making a habit of running is damned suspicious. You could've saved everyone a hell of a lot of trouble if you'd only—"

A horn blared an instant ahead of a sickening crunch as something slammed into the ambulance's rear right side. The jolt sent the vehicle sliding, then spinning out of control. The driver yelled, "Hold on!" and the EMT shrieked as the force of the impact slung her across Marcus's body.

With the ambulance still careening to the right, the officer grabbed at—and missed—the rail of Marcus's gurney. The right tires dropped hard off the pavement, and the vehicle's left side rose, shifted and finally tipped, accompanied by the sounds of screams.

Equipment flying, the heavy vehicle slammed onto its side with a deafening crash. As the rear doors popped open, the interior lights winked out.

Recovering more quickly than the others, Marcus wriggled an arm free of the strap that had held him to the gurney. Around him in the darkness, he heard the creaking and hissing of the wrecked vehicle, and the moaning of the officer, who lay sprawled below him on the side of the ambulance that now served as its floor.

The EMT's panicked voice climbed the register. "My leg. Oh, God, my leg hurts. Compound fracture—bone's sticking through the skin. Hal? You okay up there? Axel? Talk to me, Ax."

The driver groaned, "My head," and the paramedic called out, "Axel? Holcomb?"

The big cop didn't answer as, in the distance,

Marcus heard the shrill of sirens. Emergency vehicles coming to help.

Lifting his good arm, he felt the handcuff that had been locked to the gurney slip free from a broken rung. In a lightning flash, he understood that he had one chance. One miraculous opportunity to extricate himself and slip away.

With rescuers on the way, he didn't hesitate for a moment. He quickly clambered off the gurney and scrambled to the door.

Headlights shone through from one of at least four vehicles parked helter-skelter along the freeway's shoulder. Three men rushed toward him, the nearest shouting, "Everybody all right?"

Marcus looked to the right, into the darkness beyond the ambulance, which lay smoking on its side beside a drainage ditch. Swampland, alligators—anything could lie out in that direction, but still, it was his only chance.

His only shot at freedom, one he owed it to his family to take.

It was his only shot, so he aimed carefully, sighting the runner disappearing in the blackness and holding his breath to squeeze the trigger.

At the sharp crack, the bystanders who had been rushing toward the ambulance shouted, panicking. One of them fell to her knees, clutching her chest before collapsing.

Another dead, perhaps, in addition to those he might have killed when he had deliberately struck the ambulance in his desperation to kill his rival. Despite the sacrifices he'd made and the risk to his own safety, he suspected he had missed his target, for his hands were shaking and his heart pounding so hard, he doubted he could hit a billboard, let alone one runner in the night.

With the sirens drawing nearer, he slipped back into his car, congratulating himself on having demolished the ambulance with only minimal damage to his own vehicle, and sped off. Panic might have cost him the chance to kill the man seeking to deprive him of his rightful bride again, but he prayed that this time he had at least scared the bastard off for good.

Or at least for long enough that he could claim the woman who'd been born—then reborn—just for him. The flesh-and-blood version of the dolls who would surely guide him to escape all consequences for his actions.

Including those that left so many silent, glass-eyed victims in his wake.

Chapter Fifteen

Detective Davis leaned across the interview-room table, his *rougaroux* fangs and onion-tainted breath making Caitlyn sit back farther in her chair.

"You may have Reuben snowed," he said, "but I know damned well there's more to this story than you're saying."

Heart thumping, Caitlyn shoved her chair back and surged to her feet. Since he'd bludgeoned her with the news that Marcus's ambulance had crashed and Marcus was missing, she felt wild, reckless—and in absolutely no mood for anymore of this man's bullying. "Maybe you should call Detective Robinson back in, since you haven't heard a single thing I've told you."

Davis stood to face her. "You say something worth listening to, I'll listen. But you keep shoveling that bullshit, don't be shocked when I won't open wide and say *Ah*."

At the contempt in his eyes, she shook her head

in disbelief. With his partner called out of the room, he'd clearly taken off the gloves.

Was he closer to her old boss than she had imagined? Could Josiah have convinced him, maybe even bribed him, to do whatever it took to cause her grief?

"I've told you three times, I have to call Reuben," she said. "He'll be frantic when he gets back to my house and finds that broken back door."

Shaken as she'd been, she had forgotten about calling on the way here, and the moment she had stepped inside the interview room, her cell phone had lost its signal. Did they have a way of jamming calls, or was the low battery warning the problem?

"I thought he was your friend," she added.

"If you're so worried about Reuben, just come clean with me, and you can get out and call him yourself."

"What is it you want, Detective?" she demanded. "I've already explained what happened this evening at least three times, by my count."

"Guess I shouldn't be surprised you make your living telling stories," he scoffed. "That fairytale about the little old lady no one else but you can see—I'm sure the tourists would eat it all up with their silver spoons."

She rolled her eyes. "So that photo of her in the cemetery—that's a figment of my imagination?"

He waved off her question. "God only knows what you and your lover boy cooked up. What I want are the facts. The cold, hard facts about what really happened tonight and who really shot Le Carpentier."

Rather than rising to the bait, she bluffed. "I've already told you everything I know." She had no intention of admitting to her short-lived attempt at keeping Marcus captive, much less the way she'd fallen for the hero behind those hard brown eyes.

That thought startled her out of her anger at the detective, and she sucked in a sharp breath. Because it was absolutely true. In spite of every sensible reason she had to run in the opposite direction, she really had fallen for Marcus's courage and his willingness to sacrifice for those he loved, his soul, his face, that hard, well-muscled body.

She wanted him as she had never wanted any man before. Wanted to hold him, to make love with him, to spend day after day unraveling his mysteries, getting to know every facet of him. Irrational as it seemed, her eyes filled with tears as she was blindsided by images of the two of them together, playing hide and seek in the mansion with three beautiful children, two strapping, dark-haired boys and a laughing blonde toddler with chubby legs and eyes as green as grass, just like her mother's.

Impossible, she thought, and ridiculously old-fashioned, light-years from the Bohemian business-owner roadmap she'd had for her own life. Yet the vision drew her in, so vivid and sharp-edged that it sliced her to the bone. For it was a vision that could never be, of children who would never be born, a man who could never claim the right to be a husband or a father. A forlorn, hopeless future that shattered something deep inside her.

Her emotions must have bled through, because Davis closed in on her, pumping his index finger toward her chest with every furious word. "It's all over your face. You're letting that guy screw you. And you're lyin' for him, too. I'd stake my pension you know exactly where he's run to."

"Then I hope you're good at panhandling," she shot back, "because I have no idea. For all I know, he could be badly hurt. Or even—even—"

"Dead," Davis finished for her. "And that's the damned truth. If whoever tried to off him before hasn't caught up to him, the dogs'll run him to ground out there in the dark. And I can tell you, sister, all bets are off when this kind of arrest goes down at night."

Struggling to vanquish the horrific thoughts

conjured by his words, she wiped away angry tears. "Why are you doing this?"

"Because I've got a fellow cop dead in that ambulance wreck, and I'm just itching to throw anyone in jail who's been aiding and abetting the man who caused that crash."

"Detective Robinson said it was an accident."

He hesitated a few beats before shaking his head. "Nothing accidental about it, according to witnesses. Somebody rammed the rear quarter panel and caught the back tire, which spun it out. And if that wasn't enough to seal the deal, somebody—probably the same bastard—took a couple of potshots at Le Carpentier while he was running."

"What?" she cried. "Was he shot again?"

Davis's shrug said he couldn't care less. "Believe me, the cops are out there beating the bushes. 'Cause the question of the hour is who the hell's out to kill him, and how's all this connected? And the way I figure it, only you or he can tell us."

"Did you ever think of the fact that whoever murdered those two women might be out to keep him from talking? Maybe that morning in the cemetery, Marcus caught even more in his pictures than he realized. Or someone thinks he did."

"So you're tellin' me it's just a coincidence

that your guy's wanted for the murder of his own fiancée? And some mysterious *other* killer's out to shut him up? *Please,"* he scoffed.

Her need to accuse Josiah Paine warred with the instinct not to mention him to his friend Davis. Finally she said, "Bring back Detective Robinson. I'd like to speak to her. Alone."

Davis glowered at her. "You got something personal against me?"

She held his gaze. "Absolutely, Detective."

"You wanna explain that?"

She shook her head. "Not a bit. Now, will you get her, or do I end this conversation right now?"

"Let's suppose I decide to hold you, maybe leave you in the parish lockup until morning. I can see to it you have some real *interesting* company." His eyes glittered, cold as ice chips. "Pretty girl like you, you might come away with all sorts of new *friends,* not to mention some new stories. Maybe not the type you'll want to tell your tour groups, though."

Caitlyn felt a prickling behind her neck. "Then I want a lawyer," she said, though she had no idea how she would pay one. "But either way, I'm finished talking to you."

He shrugged. "Suit yourself, Miss Villaré."

With that, he turned and strode out, closing the door firmly behind himself. And leaving her to wonder whether he was going to find his partner or make good on his threat to have her jailed overnight.

She paced the room and rubbed her arms to keep from freezing in the air-conditioning. But distracting as the cold was, her worry for Marcus burned like a hot coal in her belly. Was he scared? In pain? Would they hunt him down and shoot him like a rabid animal?

Raw terror seared its way up her throat, and she fought an impulse to be sick.

Detective Robinson walked in, stopping half-way across the room before shaking her head. "Lord, girl. You could hang meat in this icebox. Let me see what I can do about that."

She disappeared for another minute before returning and passing Caitlyn a fuzzy brown cardigan, a close match to the ivory version the detective herself wore.

"That AC's got a mind of its own, but here, this'll help," she said.

Ordering herself to calm down and not give away her concern for Marcus by blurting out her questions, Caitlyn draped the oversize sweater over her trembling shoulders. "Thanks. And I'm really glad it was your turn to play Good Cop."

"I *am* a good cop." Robinson smiled, her brace-lets jingling as she settled her broad rear into the seat across from the one Caitlyn took. "Would've been a better one, though, if I'd done my homework sooner."

Caitlyn tilted her head. "Homework?"

"ViCAP—that's the federal database that helps track violent criminals—is only as good as the departments keeping the information up to date." The detective shook her head, her disapproval written in her face. "Thanks to somebody forgetting to follow up his paperwork, we never got the news about Theo Le Carpentier."

"You mean…you know he has a brother?"

Detective Davis shook her head, her light eyes darkening with some emotion. "*Had* a brother. Marcus hasn't had a brother for the past four years."

THE DOGS WERE CLOSING IN, their frenzied barking growing louder by the second.

Crouching in the damp weeds, Marcus peered out at the frontage road and prayed the ride he had called—thank God he'd managed to hold on to his cell phone—would beat the frenzied animals and their handlers, who would undoubtedly shoot first and ask questions later.

"Come on, Craven," he murmured, hating to stake his life on the motel clerk. Marcus prayed that the kid had really meant it when he'd sworn he was up for anything, and that he would prove the kind of guy who would ask no questions, not even of a sweating, bloodstained man who had arranged a ride less than a mile from the spot where the freeway had been shut down and emergency vehicles were swarming like buzzing flies on a fresh kill.

As the dogs drew steadily closer, Marcus felt the sting of what seemed like a thousand insect bites and scratches, along with the relentless throbbing of his injured arm. Blinking to clear the sweat pouring into his eyes, he squinted down the street and willed a pair of headlights to separate themselves from the sporadic traffic and pull off to the side.

Nothing. Not a damned thing. And the dogs were getting so close that he could hear the deep, excited voices of their handlers.

With nowhere to run that the animals wouldn't find him, he thought of turning himself in. Thought of tossing aside his own years of struggle, of what surrendering would mean to Theo's future. And thought, improbably, of losing his last chance to see Caitlyn, to hear her sweet voice, and feel her heart beating against his, beneath his as he...

As if she weren't lost to him already.

His groan was followed by a rush of pure determination. If he had to run on foot through traffic, to attempt to lose his pursuit in the blare of horns, the flash of lights and the smell of diesel, he would damned well do it rather than surrender. He had fought too long for his family, for his freedom, to accept defeat.

Bursting from the cover of the weeds, he charged toward the road—just as a low-slung pair of headlights careened onto the shoulder and tires squealed to a stop.

With the dogs sounding as if they might explode through the underbrush at any second, Marcus jumped inside and slammed the door shut. "Go, go!"

"Where to?" asked Craven, his narrow gaze flicking toward him.

"Anywhere, I don't care. Out of here—fast."

With a throaty rumble, the aging Camaro slipped back into the lane and glided toward safety, while Marcus caught the glint of the searchers' flashlights...lights that were rapidly left behind.

"Not *too* fast," Marcus cautioned him. "No need to attract undue attention."

As the black ribbon of the highway led them farther away from danger, Marcus's heartbeat slowed its breakneck rhythm.

Minutes later, Craven asked him, "We're away. What now?"

Marcus knew better than to try an E.R. or walk-in clinic, where the staff would waste no time in reporting a gunshot wound. "Could use some place to clean up," he said. "And some fresh clothes, while we're at it."

The driver shoved the greasy hair away from a pair of eyes as blue and innocent as any infant's. Licking his lips, he gave a quick nod. "Another two-fifty, and I can make that happen."

Marcus had the two hundred fifty, in addition to the four hundred he had already promised the guy, but very little more. Still, he was in no position to negotiate, and the entrepreneurial Craven knew it.

"Then make it happen," Marcus agreed, his mind already moving on to how he was going to get back to collect his belongings and his pickup.

And whether Caitlyn had told the police about the hidden truck.

Chapter Sixteen

With her stomach tightly knotted, Caitlyn dug in her handbag for her cell phone, hoping she had enough battery left to make a call. Though the detectives had offered her a ride home, she wanted nothing to do with the police, who even now might be shooting Marcus down like an animal.

Standing just inside the lobby, she was about to phone Natalie before remembering that her friend had taken her two-year-old daughter and left town for a few days—that she had called only this afternoon to remind Caitlyn to stop by her apartment to feed her fish and check her mail.

Though she dreaded the lecture she was sure to hear from Reuben, she tried him instead, only to have her cell battery give a single chirp before it died completely.

"Great," she murmured, glancing first at the lobby desk, where an exasperated officer was trying to calm down a crying, drunken woman who had staggered through the front door, followed by an equally intoxicated man pleading that he hadn't meant whatever it was he'd done to her. With the noise of their voices echoing around her, Caitlyn headed outdoors rather than wait to ask to use the phone.

Almost immediately, she spotted a cab, and even more miraculously, she was able to flag him down. Climbing into the backseat, she gave the driver her address before sinking into a tense silence, her mind churning with worry.

"Right there, by the front gate," she said a few minutes later, interrupting the cabbie's conversation with his dispatcher.

With an absent nod, the doughy lump of a man complied, pointing out the ticker while saying, "Yeah, sure, Reggie. I can be there in about three minutes."

Overpaying him by half, Caitlyn interrupted again. "Can you watch until I go inside, please? It'll only take a moment."

Another nod, and she stepped out of the aging cab, but no sooner did she close the door than the taxi sped away. Cursing the driver's impatience, she hurried through the gate, her heart pumping primal fear through her veins.

"It'll be fine," she told herself as she stepped through the front gate and past the spot where she had found the dead girl's body. Keys jingling, she hurried up the front steps, past the place where Eva Rill had lurked, a gun in her withered hands.

Carried on a sultry breeze, the strains of jazz floated from somewhere in the Quarter. A dog's barking echoed faintly, and from another direction, a siren's wail stretched, thin and eerie as the ghost of an old scream.

Every tiny hair on her body rising with that thought, Caitlyn thrust her key toward the lock....

And shrieked in alarm when a shadow detached itself from the space behind one of the columns—a man, this time—reaching toward her too swiftly for any hope of escape.

Twisting away from his grasp, Caitlyn reflexively struck out, thrusting her arms forward to push him away. The heel of one hand thumped his chest, and her stiffened fingers jabbed the key into his face.

"Stop!" Panic tore from the man's throat, his shout even louder that her own as he backpedaled and lost his balance. With a loud grunt, he thumped down the front steps, landing on his rear end, his bald scalp gleaming beneath the security light.

"Max?" Caitlyn cried, at last recognizing her former coworker. "Max Lafitte, what are you *doing?*"

"God, my eye! You bitch! I'm only here to—"

"To what, Max?" Caitlyn shouted, trembling

above him. "To lurk by my front door when a killer's targeted me so you can scare me to death and save him the trouble?"

"To deliver a message from Josiah, not to be assaulted by another crazy Villaré."

"What do you mean, *another?*" she demanded. "Is this about my parents? I don't have the first clue what you're talking about."

"I'm bleeding here—and I can't see anything with my left eye." His hand covering the injury and his head jerking on his scrawny neck, he looked and sounded less dangerous than pathetic.

Or was she wrong about that? Had she actually stopped a deranged killer with no weapon but a key?

"What if I lose this eye?" he continued, reminding her of the women who had lost theirs.

"Maybe you can replace it with a glass one," she accused, then ventured a bluff, at the same time unlocking the door without looking away from Max. "I understand you're partial to green."

"What's wrong with you?" he wailed. "I should sue your ass for everything you own."

Caitlyn snorted. "You want a piece of my tax lien, you've got it. And call the police, too. Be my guest. I'm sure they'll be interested in how you attempted to assault me."

Max staggered to his feet and limped backward, his head shaking. "You're outright crazy, do you know that? Every bit as insane as your—"

"Wait! You said you had a message from Josiah. You saw him?"

Lafitte kept backing away, "He says to keep your boyfriend clear of him if you don't want him to end up floating in the Mississippi, and if you don't want to end up joining—"

"When did you talk to him? When did he give you that message?"

But it was too late. Max was already hurrying toward the gate, his hand covering his eye like his namesake's pirate patch. Soon he vanished into the darkness, leaving Caitlyn to wonder how much different the outcome might have been without that single lucky jab of her key.

Inside the house, she found a hammer, nails and leftover wood from an earlier makeshift repair, and secured the broken back door as best she could before plugging her dead cell phone into its charger. Within seconds the notification chime alerted her that she had voice mail. Probably about a hundred messages from Reuben, she decided, and cut to the chase by ignoring them and calling his cell phone directly.

When he didn't answer, she left a brief message before trying his home phone. No answer there, either, which struck her as strange.

Looking for an explanation, she connected

with her voice mail. The first three messages, as she'd expected, consisted of various versions of Reuben's increasingly gruff: "Where the hell are you? I'm worried."

Expecting more of the same, she nearly hung up before a crisply efficient older woman began: "Hello, this is Laura Withers, from the Interim LSU Public Hospital Emergency Department. I'm calling for a Caitlyn Villaré. A patient brought in this evening, Mr. Reuben Pierce, is asking that we let you know he's being admitted for observation following a concussion. He insisted I tell you not to worry and that he'll be sure to call you in the morning."

"What?" Caitlyn erupted, as if the recorded message could answer all her questions. How had Reuben gotten a concussion? Had someone attacked him, as she'd been struck and knocked unconscious in the cemetery during the storm? Was someone—the real killer—targeting him the same way Marcus had been targeted?

And could the killer's point be to leave her unprotected and alone?

LONG AND DARK, the sedan parked across the street and two doors down from Caitlyn's mansion had the look of an unmarked surveillance vehicle. Squinting hard in its direction, Marcus made out the orange glow of a lit cigarette clenched in the teeth of the bulky silhouette behind the wheel.

"Keep driving," Marcus told Craven.

The kid nodded. "I saw him, too. Cops're staking out the place, man. So what now?"

"Let me think for a few minutes." Fresh from a shower, and clad in a clean though tight-fitting black T-shirt and jeans Craven had found for him, Marcus was grateful for the mild painkillers that had taken the edge off the throbbing in his arm and helped restore his focus. Going the extra mile, Craven had even brewed a pot of coffee after Marcus had passed on his offer to share a tweak—the clerk's amphetamine of choice—to keep both of them going.

He considered sending Craven to get his pickup but couldn't come up with any way to get his now-twitchy accomplice past the police without triggering suspicion. After several minutes' consideration, Marcus said disgustedly, "I have no idea. Can you just drop me at the Pink Parrot Pub?"

"You wanna drink, there's places closer."

To Marcus, the bar itself was irrelevant. Only its location mattered, but he didn't want Craven to guess where he was going and try to sell that information to anyone who asked, including Josiah Paine, who might already have someone out looking to finish what he'd started. "Just take me there. All right?"

During the short ride to Metairie, Marcus made certain he projected sullenness and defeat, rather than the sense of purpose he was feeling.

Stepping inside, in case Craven was watching, Marcus found the neighborhood pub had a friendly, raucous atmosphere, as well as cheap drinks and dressed-to-thrill women looking for a good time, several of whom grinned in his direction as they eyed him at the bar. Most of the crowd's attention, however, was riveted to the spotlight, which highlighted a big-bellied, bearded white guy who'd apparently had a few too many and was indulging in a truly unfortunate karaoke version of an old Aretha Franklin tune.

Good-natured as it was, the jeers and laughter made the place far too loud for Marcus to place his call. So after ordering a beer so as not to rouse suspicion, he slipped out into the darkness and prayed Caitlyn would be home.

As he used his prepaid cell to pull up the number he'd saved from her website, he prayed even harder that she would be willing to speak to him. And not only talk but allow him to convince her to help him make one last-ditch effort to escape New Orleans for good.

Did he even have the right to try? To risk her

freedom, possibly her life, so he could continue to keep a monster from facing the consequences of his actions?

The thought brought him up short, and not for the first time, he weighed the cost of what he was doing against the memory of the happy boy he had helped to raise.

It was the memory of that love that tipped the balance, of a duty and a responsibility that outweighed death itself. But not his concern for Caitlyn, he swore. He would find some way to keep her safe, no matter what it took.

CAITLYN TRIED PHONING THE HOSPITAL, only to learn that Reuben's name had not yet been added to the list of patients who'd given permission to provide confirmation of their presence and condition to callers. Because of federal privacy laws, the sympathetic-but-inflexible woman on the other end explained, she could offer nothing more specific than the hospital's visiting hours.

It was maddening, not knowing, so Caitlyn tried calling Lorna Robinson to see if she could find out anything about what had landed Reuben in the hospital, though she was personally convinced it had been an attack. But the detective's voice mail picked up, playing a message that explained she was off-duty and would return calls in the morning.

"If your needs cannot wait," the recording advised, "please hang up and dial 9-1-1."

"I *can't* wait!" Caitlyn burst out before disconnecting, but she knew better than to dial the emergency number over what would undoubtedly be considered a trivial concern.

She took a deep breath and counted to ten, reminding herself that Reuben, who was as big and tough as they came, had gone out of his way to get a message to her telling her not to worry.

"So why didn't you leave some instructions telling me how?" she asked the empty room before Sinister poked his fluffy head into the kitchen to eye her reproachfully.

When the office phone rang, she hurried to answer in the hope Reuben had decided to call her after all. In her rush, she grabbed it without glancing at the Caller ID, a decision she regretted the moment she heard Josiah Paine's voice.

"What'd you do to Lafitte?" he shouted so loudly that she had to pull the phone a foot from her ear.

"Did you send Max to hurt me?"

"Lafitte?" Paine nearly choked on laughter. "Believe me, if I wanted you dead, I've got friends better equipped for the job, you stupid bimbo. Friends who can handle you and Reuben Pierce and that jackass who tried to jump me outside my own business."

"You shot him," Caitlyn accused before adding, because she knew Josiah, "And you shot him for no reason."

"No reason, my fat keister. That maniac threatened me to get me to stay away from you. Told me he'd *destroy* me if I even thought of bothering you. And anyone who saw the look in his eyes would swear on a stack of Bibles he meant what he was saying."

Caitlyn pictured that intense look. Shivered at the thought of Marcus's dark eyes heating with an equally fierce passion as they gazed at *her*.

The thought of that gaze forever dimming made her snap at her ex-boss, "I can see you were intimidated by the way you're calling me at midnight, threatening me again."

"Not *you,* I'm not," Paine qualified, anxiety making his voice more nasal. "If you talk to him, you make sure that's a hundred percent clear."

"So that means no more dead girls, Josiah? No more threats from Max or your pals or horrible old women showing up to try to kill me?"

"What the hell craziness are you talking, Caitlyn? I told you, I have nothing to do with those poor girls, and you probably know old ladies aren't my style."

Caitlyn rolled her eyes, forcibly reminded of the dark-haired stripper he had taken up with after ditching his brassy-but-big-hearted wife of thirty-six years.

"You honestly think," he went on, "that I'm the kind of sicko who'd do something like he did with their eyes?"

She ignored his outraged horror to zero in on one huge question.

"How do *you* know about the glass eyes, Josiah? The police told me they weren't releasing that bit of information."

"It—it was Lafitte who told me," Paine stammered. "Or maybe I heard it from one of those cops I hang out with. Who knows? What does it matter? You aren't—you aren't recording this call, are you?"

"What if I am?" she bluffed.

"Wha—you're kidding, aren't you?"

She could almost hear the big jerk mentally backtracking, going over what incriminating words he might have used.

"You know I'd never really want to get anybody hurt," he said.

"Like you hurt Mar—my friend?" she corrected, not wanting to give Josiah Marcus's name.

"Listen, a man's gotta defend himself when he's threatened—I mean *assaulted*. Your boyfriend hit me, tried to *kill* me. Did I tell you that part?"

"Sure he did." If Caitlyn hadn't been so worried about Marcus and Reuben, she would have been absolutely giddy at hearing Josiah squirm.

"And I *certainly* would *never* want to take the *law* into my own hands," he said, enunciating clearly for the supposed tape. "I was only—it was just talk, you know?"

"Oh, absolutely. Exactly like your threats against me outside the post office this afternoon."

"I never—oh, hell," Paine said before hanging up, defeated.

The phone rang again only a few seconds later.

Picking it up, she said, "You should quit while you're ahead, Josiah. I'm sharing every word of this with the one cop I know who isn't in your pocket."

A stunned silence drifted through the open connection, a silence tempered by faint strains of music in the background. A moment later... "Caitlyn?"

At the single, anguished word, tears sprang to her eyes. "Marcus!" she cried. "Marcus, I've been out of my mind worrying you were dead. What happened? Are you hurt? Where are you?"

Another hesitation, then he murmured, "You've been talking to Paine?"

"He called to threaten you if you came anywhere near this city again. Whatever you do, be very careful. He's a dangerous man once provoked."

Marcus's voice dropped to a low rumble. "So he proved with his gun. But he's the one who should be scared."

She sighed at his male bluster. After everything that had happened to him, surely he must know the kind of danger he was in. "Maybe you should be, too. I heard from the police that someone shot at you again tonight after your ambulance crashed. Did he hit you? Were you hurt in the wreck?"

"I'll be fine," he promised. "What about you, Caitlyn? Are you all right? The police give you any trouble?"

"Nothing I couldn't handle," she said, her heart squeezing at the thought of what Detective Robinson had told her about Marcus's brother. Had Marcus known and lied about it, or was she about to shatter his world as he knew it? "I have to see you. We need to talk as soon as possible."

"I can't come there. They're watching your place."

"Who is?" she asked.

"The cops, I think, or maybe Reuben. There's someone waiting in a big sedan just down the street."

"It has to be the police. Reuben's in the hospital."

"What happened?"

"I wish I knew," she answered. "A nurse called

to let me know he's under observation for a concussion and that he'll call me in the morning."

"So you're alone at the house? With the murderer who's stalking you still out there?"

Wincing, she shot back, "Thanks, Marcus. I was just sitting here thinking how sleep is overrated."

"Clearly you can't stay there. But I can't come to you, so you need to take the truck and lose whoever's out there. Can you do that? *Will* you?"

Reflexively, she shook her head, her stomach flipping at the thought of leaving the safety of this refuge. But was she really safe here? Or, as Marcus had reminded her, was she a sitting duck for the same sick killer who had left two mutilated bodies for her to find, including the one on her front lawn?

Could he, rather than the police, be the man waiting and watching out front in his car?

The man waiting for her to switch the lights off before he moved in to finish the deadly game that he had started...

Chapter Seventeen

Such a strange place to meet a woman, where strands of moonlight pierced the wispy clouds and restless spirits wandered row after row of the mausoleums housing the dust of their remains.

Strange and somewhat dangerous, yet tonight Marcus had been drawn to Metairie Cemetery, a place he had so far avoided, though it was one of the most beautiful and storied in New Orleans. He'd steered clear mostly out of fear that if he stopped by *her* tomb, he would never again be able to photograph the others without the thought of his mother's grave blotting out their images.

There it was, just as he remembered. Her name, Eva Dauphin Le Carpentier, inscribed above "Beloved Wife and Mother" and the tragically brief span of her life. She didn't have the tomb, an oven-style bank crowned by an open book and a laurel wreath, to herself but shared eternity with her parents, grandparents and a few other lost relations.

She had been the last of them, save for the three children and the hard-drinking husband she had left behind.

Why? Why did you leave your kids with a drunken father? And what the hell am I supposed to do about our family now?

In the questions' wake, guilt rolled in, flooding his conscience with regret. So he turned away, striding among the chorusing insects and toward the back gate where he had promised to meet Caitlyn.

Though he had seen and heard no one since his arrival, his senses remained attuned to the slightest stirring of the light breeze, the subtlest flickering of the shadows.

Twelve minutes passed, stretching his anxiety to the breaking point, because Caitlyn should have been there by this time. Had she been arrested attempting to elude the officer outside her house? Or, more frightening still, had she been caught on her way to the detached garage by a murderer lurking nearby, eager for such a golden opportunity?

And what of the brief but potentially dangerous walk from where she would have to park the truck to this spot? Shifting his position, he struggled to watch from every angle, to keep his vow to see her through this safely.

He strode past a temple-like tomb, sick with

the visions taking shape in his imagination, dark memories of his murdered fiancée, her body bearing Caitlyn's face. Tasting bile, he ripped the phone out of his pocket, only to feel it fly from his hand.

Relieved when it landed on grass rather than concrete, he bent to pick it up, then jerked his head toward a sound. A blur of movement caught his eye just beyond the back gate.

He released the breath he had been holding. "Caitlyn?"

"Marcus," she called back. "How do I get in? Oh, I see."

Rushing toward her, he helped her push aside the broken fence so she could squeeze inside.

"I was so damned worried I'd gotten you killed." He pulled her into a hard, possessive embrace as she wrapped her arms around him. Pain flared in his injured arm, but he shoved it aside. "I don't know what I'd do if something happened to you."

She cupped his face in her hands and looked into it, her eyes only inches from his. "Talk about scaring someone. I thought I'd never see you aga—"

He covered her mouth with his own, feeding his hunger for a woman he could never get enough of. She murmured in protest before melting against him in surrender to the moment. From deep in her throat, he heard a small moan, a sound that had him aching to give and take every pleasure their bodies had to offer.

There was an almost-painful urgency in the meeting of their mouths, the slick touch of their tongues against each other, and the way their hands skimmed curve and plane alike, his hard muscle and her velvet softness. But all too soon it ended, with Caitlyn breaking off the kiss and pushing him away to say, "No, we can't. They're watching."

Reflexively, he whirled around, ready to fight whatever intruder offered either threat or interruption. Then he stopped, embarrassed to remember where they were and *who* was looking on.

The dead were all around them. He felt their presence as they watched from behind the bricked-off windows and iron grates of tombs and mausoleums. And he felt, or imagined that he did, the mix of curiosity and disapproval from behind their sightless eyes.

"You're right," he said. "It's disrespectful. I just forget myself around you."

But Caitlyn was shaking her head, turning to point out a pair of dark silhouettes emerging from behind a tomb, reminding Marcus that the living posed a far greater threat to their survival than the dead.

CAITLYN TOOK AN INVOLUNTARY STEP BACKWARD as the light of the full moon washed over a pair of haggard, unshaved faces. Already shaky from her struggle to elude the dark car tailing her from her place, she'd barely given a thought to the vagrants that sometimes turned to the dubious shelter of the cemeteries.

Marcus stepped in front of her as the two gaunt men approached, coming so close she could smell their gamey reek.

"Got cash on you?" slurred a dark-skinned man with gray hair. "Could use a couple burgers and maybe one more six-pack."

"You'll want to back off," Marcus warned, his stance squaring and his muscles tensing. "You step away, and we'll talk."

Instead, the younger man, his bald head scabby, moved in closer and craned his skinny neck to look Caitlyn up and down. "Girl's got herself a purse there. Come and share what you got, sweetie. *All* you got."

At their suggestive laughter, Marcus withdrew a folded bill from his jeans and warned, "I'm giving you two choices. Back off with a twenty and have yourselves a pleasant evening, or hobble off with my shoe leather jammed between your cheeks."

What came next happened so fast, Caitlyn barely saw it. As the first man stooped to grab the money Marcus let flutter to the ground, the second pulled a blade from somewhere, a movement she recognized only in swift blur of reflected moonlight.

Marcus moved even faster, spinning sideways in a roundhouse kick that cracked against the attacker's wrist and sent the knife clattering off a tombstone. With a sharp cry, the man grasped his injured forearm and lumbered back into the shadows. The gray-haired man took off in the opposite direction with the money clutched tightly to his chest.

"Funny," said Marcus, grinning, "he doesn't seem much into sharing with his friend, either."

Her relief morphed into anger. "That man—he could have killed us, and you're *enjoying* this?"

He shook his head. "Not really. I don't like to hurt the homeless, and I was wrong to put us in this situation."

"So why did you?" she asked him.

He sighed. "I'm sorry. I've been asking myself the same question. But my mother's buried here, and as much as it hurts to see her grave, I…I couldn't bring myself to leave without saying goodbye."

The sadness in his voice extinguished her anger like a lit match. She slipped her hand into his. "Did you get the chance to see her?"

"I did. But I'm afraid she's fresh out of advice about dealing with my brother."

Caitlyn felt of pang of foreboding. Clearly he had no idea his brother was dead. How would it affect him, hearing it on this already hellish night?

"Let's go for a ride," she suggested. "The truck's not far."

He nodded. "We need to get out of here anyway, before we have more company than I can deal with."

"Speaking of which," she said, as she preceded him through the gate, "where'd you learn to fight like that? You looked like Chuck Norris or somebody."

He laughed, shaking his head, and squeezed through the gap behind her. "Not quite, but let's just say a guy living on the lam picks up what he needs to know to keep himself in one piece. To me, the greatest strength is avoiding conflict whenever possible."

As they walked toward the parked truck, she tried to memorize his clean scent and the comforting weight of his hand at her waist. Tried to draw whatever comfort she could from being in his presence.

An instant later the sound of gunfire shattered

the illusion, bullets zinging off the pavement and punching through the sheet metal of the truck's rear panel.

Chapter Eighteen

Marcus grabbed for Caitlyn, and she went down beside him with a shriek.

He dragged her toward the passenger door and wrenched it open, shoving her inside. "Head down!" he shouted, as another gunshot took out the back window.

Caitlyn crunched her way across the glass-strewn bench seat, then jammed the keys into the ignition as he swung in behind her.

As the door slammed shut, the Dodge's big engine roared to life. Their tires squealed as Caitlyn floored the accelerator and pulled away from the curb.

Marcus looked her over, relieved to see no blood but unable to be certain in the dim light. "You okay? Were you hit?"

"Not hit," she said, "but my heart feels like it's about to explode. Who was shooting? Did you see? One of those homeless guys?"

Marcus shook his head. "The shots were coming from the street, I think."

He looked behind them, through the shattered rear window, his fears confirmed when he spotted a pair of headlights swiftly approaching. He was certain it was the dark sedan that belonged to whoever had been watching the front of Caitlyn's house.

Her gaze flicking to the rearview, she obviously drew the same conclusion, because she said, "Oh, no. I thought for sure I'd lost him. I'm so sorry. I must have led him straight here."

"We'll get rid of him," Marcus told her. "Turn off your headlights and keep going."

"It's dark out here. We'll crash."

"Let me guide you," he assured her. "I grew up around here. My sister and I used to ride our bikes on these streets."

Rimmed with white, her eyes darted toward him. "Did you used to ride them at sixty miles an hour in the pitch dark? With some maniac with a *gun* behind you?"

"Calm down," he said. "Calm down, and we'll get through this."

"Calm *down?*" she asked, as if he were insane.

But maybe he was, he decided as he said, "It all boils down to this. Do you trust me, Caitlyn? Will you trust me with our lives?"

NEARLY AN HOUR LATER, Caitlyn was still shaking, certain that at any moment shots would follow them into Natalie's apartment, in a partitioned-off old house in a mostly resurrected neighborhood not far outside the Quarter. Marcus had pulled the truck behind the building, wanting to keep it close by in case they had to make a quick escape.

"No one will find us here," she repeated for at least the fifth time, more to reassure herself than Marcus, who was sitting on the sofa beside her in a room lit only by the watery glow of a large saltwater aquarium. As the blue and yellow and orange-striped fish swam in lazy circles, his uninjured arm was draped over her for comfort.

Yet the longer she sat there, nervously watching the closed curtains for unfamiliar shadows and jumping when the air-conditioning kicked on, the more her mind gave way to visions of an armed man kicking in the front door, spraying gunfire over the room where she had so often stopped by to chat with Natalie or play with her daughter, Kylie. As her eyes closed, nightmare images flashed through her mind: the stuffing exploding, from Kylie's shot-up teddy bear, the aquarium glass shattering with the impact, and Marcus sliding to the floor, a far more terrifying outcome than if she'd been struck herself.

Gasping, Caitlyn jerked awake, gasping as if she'd run a footrace.

"It's okay. Everything's fine," Marcus told her. "You only dozed off for a minute, but you're safe. We really lost him."

Her gaze met his, and in his eyes she saw the strain of worry, the weight of the pain he hadn't mentioned as he watched over her in the dark. But she saw strength, too, strength and courage he was more than willing to allow her to rely on.

"How 'bout something to drink?" he asked her. "Water? Soda? Maybe your friend has something stronger in the kitchen?"

She shook her head, trusting him to feel the movement. "No. I need to stay right here, just like this."

It felt safe. *He* felt safe to her, though she knew that beyond this oasis of calm, there were no guarantees for either of them.

"Then let's stay a little longer." Warm and solid, his arm tightened around her. "No one will be looking for us here."

She sighed, drawing on his strength for a few more minutes before guilt made her restless. Sitting up, she kept one hand to his chest. "There's something…something I wanted to tell you— before the shooting started."

Beside her, he straightened. "What is it, Caitlyn? Whatever it is, I can take it."

Though she'd gone over it a dozen times in her head, she couldn't think of a gentle way to ease into such a brutal subject. So she said it plainly, as calmly and compassionately as she could manage. "Detective Robinson says your brother's dead. That he's been dead for four years."

"*What?* They're wrong. Like I told you, he's in a private care facility." Anger dropped his words to a growl. "Damned cops are using you. Using you to mess with my head."

"He was shot by a security guard as he left a condo where somebody triggered a panic alarm." Touching his arm, she added quietly, "They found the resident, Marcus…a young woman who'd been strangled. And your brother had set fires on his way out, in the bedroom where the body—"

"He wasn't shot killing Samantha. He escaped. I saw him after, before I—"

Caitlyn shook her head. "That's not who I mean, Marcus. I'm telling you he was shot after murdering a second woman, a short time after you left."

"*No.* That's bullshit. There *was* no second woman. We put Theo in a safe place. My sister checks in on him twice a month. And heaven knows I've paid enough all these years to keep him—"

"The police in your hometown—they know he killed Samantha, too. After Theo died, they compared the DNA, but somehow the department's discovery was never entered into the federal database, so when the New Orleans PD looked, they saw you were wanted in connection—"

"They're lying." Anguish roared through his voice. "Making this all up to get me to let my guard down. Theo couldn't have… He's in a good place, a safe place where he'll always be well treated. There's even a chance that he'll get better, a new medicine that might help."

She wanted nothing more than to drag Marcus into her arms, to comfort him and tell him he was right, and the cops had it all wrong. But she wouldn't lie to him, not even to ease his pain.

Instead, she asked a simple question. "When was the last time you spoke to your brother?"

"We don't speak anymore. We tried it once on the phone, and he became so agitated that…"

Beside her on the sofa, Marcus leaned forward, his elbows on his knees and his head in his hands. Seeing him in such pain, regret spiked through her. Once more she was seized with the desire to take everything back.

Instead, she asked, "When, Marcus? When did you last hear your brother's voice?"

He considered, then shrugged. "Maybe a week or two after…after Samantha. Then Stacey said I shouldn't call. She said—oh, God, not Stacey. My little sister couldn't— She would never…"

"You brought in a backpack from the truck, right?" she asked, relieved that they had grabbed it from where he'd left it behind the seat. "Is your laptop in there?"

He nodded mutely, his jaws clenched so tightly she half expected to hear the crack of fractured teeth.

"Let's double check this, just to be sure. Maybe we can log onto Natalie's wireless network, if we can figure out the password."

"That's no problem. I've got a satellite account," he murmured as he reached for the bag.

Caitlyn didn't dare speak as he powered up the machine and logged onto the web.

With a search engine open and his brother's name typed into the "find" box, Marcus hesitated, his finger hovering above the enter key. Hovering and shaking.

"I check for my own name from time to time, just to see if there's any news related to a manhunt." He turned his wounded gaze toward her. "But it was just too painful, looking for Samantha's. The one time I did, I came across a tribute page, and… I never hunted for my brother. I thought I knew where he was."

She laid her hand over his. "It's time, Marcus. Time to learn the truth, whatever it is."

One fingertip atop the other, they pushed the "enter" button together.

And in two clicks found confirmation of everything the detective had told her.

Chapter Nineteen

Summed up in the *Pittsburgh Post-Gazette*'s news archives, the facts had a finality that made the blood drain from Marcus's face.

"I'm so sorry." Caitlyn's words came as a dim echo, a message of comfort from a distant galaxy.

Four years. Theo had been dead for almost exactly four years.

And worse yet, he had killed again, which meant, Marcus realized, that his sister had continued trying to care for their younger brother on her own to save money. To *steal* money, in spite of their decision and what Theo had done to Samantha. In spite of how he'd shattered Marcus's own life.

Stacey might as well have murdered the second victim herself, a young mother whose toddler daughter had been asleep in the next room. And she would have died, too, had she not been rescued before the fire spread.

Just as surely, Stacey's selfishness had cost

their brother *his* life, as well. A life that, damaged as it was, they had both been sworn to safeguard.

He thought of their last conversation, how she had pushed him for more money for Theo's care. How she always came up with exactly the right thing to tell him—like her story about the promising new medication, one just shy of FDA approval.

He swore viciously before he burst out, "*Stacey*—it's been my sister all along. Lying to me. Using me for money. Telling me the funds had to flow through her to keep me safe. The only—*only*—family I have in the whole world, and she…"

Betrayed me. Betrayed all of us…

Caitlyn shook her head, her green eyes rimmed with moisture. "I can't imagine how horrible this must be for you."

"Right before the murder, Stacey found out she was pregnant. Her boyfriend ran off to work overseas—never heard from the deadbeat again. And she'd lost her scholarship to school, too. She must've thought she couldn't make it, couldn't keep the baby, without—"

Caitlyn squeezed his hand until she got his attention.

"There's absolutely no excuse for what she did to you. No matter what her situation was."

Fierceness underscored her words, her expression telling him that if Stacey were to turn up right now, the normally gentle storyteller had enough warrior in her to rip his sister's heart out.

For his part, he hoped never to see Stacey's face again, or hear her lie her way through another conversation. His sole regret was for her daughter, a little girl doomed to grow up with a selfish liar for a mother.

Marcus wondered, too, about his brother's final actions. What had been going on in his mind, that he would attack another woman? Had he slipped out and seen a stranger who reminded him of Samantha? Or had he enjoyed that first killing so much that he'd grown fixated on repeating the experience?

Even if Theo had lived, Marcus doubted his brother would have been able to explain the impulses that moved him, impulses more mysterious and less natural than the moon's pull on the tides.

Gently and carefully, Caitlyn pushed down the lid of his laptop and moved the computer to the coffee table in front of them. "I think you've had enough for now. Maybe you should try to rest, *unless...*"

At that unfinished sentence, their gazes came together like magnets, with an almost-audible click.

"Unless I could get you something," she added,

rising to take a step toward the kitchen. "Do you need aspirin for your arm, or are you hungry, maybe? I'm sure Natalie has something in the house."

"Yes," he whispered in answer as he took her hand and gently pulled her back to the soft cushions beside him. "There *is* one thing, Caitlyn. Something I've been wanting ever since I met you."

As she settled on the sofa, her eyes flared with awareness, reflecting the blue water from across the room. In the depths of her dark pupils, he saw the tiny fish swimming swift as thought beneath the current of her tension. A current that was primed, expectant, as she grew cognizant of the turn of conversation.

The moment drew out, lengthened, like a gossamer strand of spider silk lifting on a breeze. In that charged hush, she nodded, a movement so subtle it was barely perceptible.

Marcus reacted at once, grabbing her shoulders with both hands and pulling her close enough to claim a kiss. Wanting desperately to lose himself completely, to find a place of shelter from the turmoil raging inside him.

From the moment their mouths met, passion arced through the connection. He lost track of pain, of where he was, even *who* he was, as her hand stroked his chest beneath the stretched fabric of his T-shirt. Taking her move for permission to do the same, he began to explore the slender curves that had been driving him insane for days.

As he trailed kisses down her neck, he unhooked the front closure of her bra. She tipped back her head, her catlike, closed-eyed smile and soft moan all the encouragement he needed to peel back the soft cotton and feast on the taut buds of her small but perfect breasts.

Caitlyn arched her back, raw tension pouring from her as she sighed with pleasure. Desperate to see, to touch, to taste more, he undressed her completely, making short work of her top, her capris, the silky-soft bikini panties....

Then he took the time to kiss every inch that he exposed, finally moving between her legs to bring her to a shuddering climax, his name torn from her lips almost before he'd started.

But he wasn't finished yet, not by half. Inflamed by her response, he pulled off his own clothing, freeing a rock-hard erection that had Caitlyn gasping, "Yes, please, Marcus. Please hurry. I need to...need to feel you..."

Every remaining bit of self-control shattered, the pieces raining down around them as he took her there on the couch, then took her a second time with the two of them sliding down to the rug. There was nothing slow or gentle in their coupling, nothing but the power of raw instinct, the need to vanquish past and present, to forget the impossibility of any future as he poured all his pent-up tension into the moist heat of her body and heard his shout of passion mingle with her cry.

When they were finally both spent, they lay there in stunned silence. In all too short a time, he felt the worry stealing back into his body, his muscles tensing one by one. When he felt Caitlyn, too, begin to stiffen, he suspected that, like him, she must be realizing the enormity of what they'd just done, the insanity of her surrender to a man without a single thing to offer…a man who'd forgotten himself—and Samantha's father's threat against his life—so completely that he hadn't even thought about the risk that he might leave her pregnant and alone.

THEY WOULD IMAGINE themselves safe by now. He knew it. Felt it as clearly as he felt his building fury.

Because after he'd risked so much to separate her from her guardians, Villaré had once more claimed his bride and spirited her away.

Only this time he was no rank kid intimidated by a rich man, a kid so pathetic he hadn't even fought for his fiancée.

This time he was taking back what was his, killing anyone who dared to stand in his way.

And this time his beautiful blond lover would damned well pay the price of her betrayal.

At the sound of an electronic beep, he tapped the brakes, slowing to a stop in the quiet residential street. At first he saw nothing, but once he backed up, his headlights glinted off the chrome bumper of a vehicle parked behind the old Victorian house—a house whose faded blue paint took him back to the very first house in his memory, the one where Grandmother's dolls came into his life. Came to life to advise him, to offer the friendship a lonely boy lacked...

This house was far larger than that long-ago shack, with multiple entrances that told him the old structure had been cut up into apartments. In some of them windows glowed with light, light that whispered that someone had come home. A wicked smile pulled at his lips as he wondered if one of those someones drove the old pickup... beat up except for that shining bumper someone must have recently replaced.

A bumper to which he had been wise enough to attach a tracking device as a measure of insurance before he'd lain in wait outside the cemetery.

CAITLYN'S EYES FLASHED OPEN in the near-darkness, a darkness deepened by the knowledge of exactly what she'd done.

I've fallen in love.

Or had she fallen down a hole with no escape? A flush of heat brought with it a bloom of sudden perspiration. Feeling trapped, she wriggled from beneath the heavy arm that held her and climbed to her feet, still nude.

Looking down at the well-formed muscles of Marcus's bare chest and powerful thigh, she felt a pang of loss overriding pure, animal hunger. Regret deepened when his dark eyes slitted open and he smiled like a rousing lion, surveying her from head to toe—his personal gazelle.

Reaching out for her, he offered a wordless yet unmistakable invitation. *Let's pretend a little longer....*

Shaking her head, she blinked back welling tears. "I can't do this, Marcus. Shouldn't have done it in the first place."

He moved from the rug back to the sofa, his wince betraying the cost of the sudden movement to his bandaged arm. "Ow, forgot about that. *You* made me forget...."

"You made *me* forget, too," she said. "Forget this is impossible. *We're* impossible."

In the long pause that followed, they heard noises from the neighborhood: the passing of a vehicle, the deep-throated barking of a dog.

"You could be right," he finally admitted. "But

if we both want more, if we both work for it, maybe there's still some way."

Feeling herself blush with her awareness of her nudity, Caitlyn shook her head. "There's so much to get past, Marcus. For one thing, the police still want to question you about the murders and the accident tonight. Detective Davis seems so fixated on his theory that you must have been involved, even if he has to insist you must have had an accomplice to explain it. He won't listen to you."

"I'll make him see the truth. Make all of them understand I was just a man in the wrong place at the wrong time. I'll explain why I was there, in that cemetery at that hour."

"So you *are* a professional photographer?"

He nodded. "That's right. I'm, ah, assisting with a series on funerary art. I can give them the name of the gentleman I work with. You, too, if that's what it takes to make you believe."

"I *do* believe you, Marcus. I've believed in you for some time. I couldn't help but believe."

"Then why's it so impossible to imagine we might have more than one night?"

She faltered through a smile. "I suppose you mean other than the psychopath who's been shooting at us both?"

"I'll find him, stop him somehow." Marcus

promised, his voice rumbling with a dark determination.

Caitlyn felt her heart melting just a little more. Still, she was afraid for him. "What about your fiancée's father? You said yourself he'll kill you,"

"It's worth the risk. *You're* worth whatever risks it takes to fix this."

Still, she shook her head, gathering her cropped pants and tee to hide her nakedness, to hide her fear that loving her could cost him his life. "I have a lot of things to work out, too. Too many."

"Like what, Caitlyn? Tell me, what's pushing you away?"

"We have a legacy, my sister Jacinth and I. The bequest might look like a grand one, but the mansion's nothing but a money pit. Even if we somehow scrape together the funds to pay the back taxes before the place is seized, we'll be digging ourselves out of the hole for years to come. The place needs a new roof and plumbing and every kind of repair you can imagine. I'll be working all the time, doing everything I can to make sure my business turns a profit—providing it recovers from what's been happening this week."

"Have you ever thought of leaving it? Leaving everything and jumping into your car—"

Caitlyn laid a hand over her heart. "May her rusting bones rest in peace."

Marcus smiled. "Or how about jumping in the front seat of an old Dodge pickup and heading out on the road? Keeping one step ahead of whatever trouble Samantha's father might cause."

Caitlyn let her imagination take her on an endless highway, rootless, seeing the world unspool before them. Sitting beside Marcus, never knowing where they would rest their heads come nightfall, but certain that wherever it might be, their evening would explode with sweet, mind-blowing sex.

But unlike the fantasy she'd had of Marcus and their children playing in the mansion, this one didn't feel real. It had no form or substance, contained no stories in the making. No sister nearby. No Crescent City thrumming through her blood, her very soul.

"No," she told him simply. "I won't run with you. I can't. I have a responsibility to my sister, to my father and grandfather, and every Villaré who ever lived in that house before us."

He nodded his approval. "Your family matters to you."

"Would you...*respect* me if they didn't?" Her face heated anew at the realization that she had been about to use the word *love*.

"I have nothing but respect for you," Marcus said sincerely. "Enough that I'd risk anything."

But out of fear for his safety, she was already

turning from him, saying, "I'm off to try the shower."

"We're not finished talking."

She shook her head. "I need to clean up and get dressed. It'll be light in a few hours, and I want to be waiting at the hospital to see Reuben."

"Caitlyn."

"I'll be right out," she said before she turned and walked away from him, from them. From a dream so precious to her that she couldn't risk imagining it had the slightest chance of coming true.

WHAT INFURIATED MARCUS was the sound of the lock clicking behind her. Locking him out so she could think in privacy.

But she was right, he knew, smart to distance herself from a man she clearly considered a mistake to be forgotten so she could return to her real life.

He pulled on his clothing, and stalked into the kitchen to splash water on his face and shove his hair from his eyes. There was a groan in the old pipes, and he could hear the shower running.

Washing every trace of him from Caitlyn's gleaming body.

He banished the image, cursing himself and wishing he had thought—that his brain had engaged for the few seconds it would have taken to pull a condom from his wallet. Caitlyn had made it clear she wanted no entanglements, and he wasn't the type to risk leaving an unwanted child in his wake.

Whether she wanted him around or not, he would find some way to keep tabs on her, to make certain that no kid of his arrived to feel unloved or unwelcome, even for an instant.

Maybe once he resolved his issues back in Pennsylvania, assuming he survived Samantha's father, he could even try to—

As he stared out the dark back window, a movement interrupted his thoughts. Shading his eyes to focus his attention, he confirmed it. Something—some*one*—was inside his truck, though he was absolutely certain he had locked it.

He looked around the kitchen for a potential weapon and chose a six-inch blade from the knife block. Against a bullet, it would do nothing, but, he assured himself, he was most likely dealing with a petty thief hoping to find some stray cash or a GPS he could hock, not the twisted killer of young women. And not the man—most likely one of Josiah Paine's leg breakers—who had twice tried to kill him tonight.

At least he prayed that was the case, as he crept toward the front door. Before slipping out that way so he could surprise the thief in the backyard, he hesitated for a moment, then decided that knocking on the bathroom door, shouting over the running water, might alert the person outside. Better to deal with the trouble quickly, using the element of surprise.

Slipping outdoors, he quietly closed the front door behind him. His focus narrowing to the potential dangers of the situation, he melted into the darkness armed with nothing but stealth, determination and a single borrowed blade.

Chapter Twenty

When Caitlyn emerged from the bathroom, she didn't find Marcus on the sofa. Nor did she come across him in the kitchen, though a brief glance out the window told her that the truck was still there.

After rushing through the apartment and checking both small bedrooms, she realized he was nowhere inside. Slipping on her sandals, she rushed back to the kitchen, not knowing where else he might have left a note.

Or had her rejection hurt him too badly for him to give her even that much? Had he simply walked away from her, drifting away like smoke on the wind?

Panic clawing at her throat, she couldn't even cry out his name. Couldn't find the words to apologize for her foolish attempt to push him away, despite the instincts of her heart.

And then she realized that the dome light was on in the pickup and someone was inside. She released a long sigh, relieved beyond measure that he was only readying the vehicle for their departure.

Or *his* departure, she thought, her stomach clenching at the thought that he might be leaving without even saying goodbye. Ending a relationship she had so forcefully reminded him had no chance.

But that didn't mean she could bear watching him drive away. Heart beating in a panicked rhythm, she hurried out the back door, toward the truck where—

"What on earth?" she asked, realizing that the thing moving inside the truck's cab wasn't Marcus. Wasn't even human.

It was a dog. A big, frantic, yellow Lab mix running back and forth across the bench seat, and periodically stopping to dig and whine at one door or the other.

She heard the dog crying, and then it barked desperately as it caught sight of her. Plunking its huge paws against the window, it scratched with such fervor that despite her confusion about how it could have gotten in there, she hurried to let it out.

With a yelp, the animal burst past her the minute she opened the door, collar tags jingling as it raced away—presumably heading home—

with its tail between its legs. Pushed backward by the big dog's passage, Caitlyn stumbled.

Stumbled and collided with something large and powerful that had stolen up behind her to clap a hand over her mouth before she could even draw breath for a horror-movie scream.

MARCUS NEVER KNEW WHAT HIT HIM as he stepped around the corner of the bungalow, never even knew he'd *been* hit until the moment he opened his eyes to see a pair of skinny teenage boys crouched next to him, their impossibly long limbs folded like the legs of a grasshopper.

"This what got you, mister?" he asked.

Marcus blinked and squinted, and the twin figures came together, merging into a single boy in running shorts, his dark skin marred by acne and his big hand holding a branch as thick as his wrist. As Marcus's vision swam into focus, the silvery predawn light showed blood and a few of his own hairs embedded in the bark.

As badly as his skull throbbed, he wouldn't have been surprised to see brain matter there, as well. The pain intensified as his gaze flicked to the blaze of dawn lending color to a greasy smear of sky.

Which meant, he realized, that he must have been out for…how long? Two hours? Maybe three?"

"Caitlyn," he moaned. "Where's Caitlyn?"

Oblivious, the boy explained, "My track team homeboy Darius, he run down to his house to call for help. They send an amb'lance any minute. The 5-0, too, I 'magine."

At this reference to the police, Marcus tried to stand but wobbled back down onto the grass. "Need to find her right now. Find out if she's still in Apartment 1B."

If she's still alive, he thought, fear clawing at his gut. Because if Caitlyn had been able to, surely she would have come out and found him long before this. *What if she* had *come out, if his assailant had struck him merely to lure her into the open?*

When Marcus tried to rise again, the teenager pressed down on his shoulder. "You stay right here. I get your girl for you."

Marcus tracked the progress of the boy's white running shoes as he jogged out of sight, and listened to him hammering on the apartment door for several minutes.

"She might not answer!" he called, though it made his head throb even more. "Stick your head inside and tell her Marcus needs her."

He listened as the boy called, "Miz Caitlyn? Your man need you. Marcus hurt out here. He need you to come help him."

The kid jogged back a minute later. "She not answering. Don't think she in there. Awful quiet."

"Can you give me a hand?" Marcus asked him. "I need to make sure whoever hit me didn't hurt her, too."

The boy took a full step backward, looking nervous. Flashing his pale palms, he said, "Listen, mister. Cops'll be here any minute, and I don't want to get caught up in your business. 'Specially not with somebody mean enough to beat a man down with a stick."

Marcus struggled to his feet but would have fallen had the boy not, however reluctantly, caught him by the arm. Marcus yelped, a shock of pain from his gunshot wound rocketing through him.

Letting go, the kid turned toward the street. "Sorry, man. I'm sorry. I gotta get back to my run."

Marcus thanked him, suspecting the teenager not only feared whoever had hit him but also getting blamed by the police, especially given the difference in the colors of their skin.

He staggered toward the front door, his concern firmly on Caitlyn. Had she failed to answer out of fear, or was she inside but hurt—or worse?

He went in shouting her name, then stumbled through the apartment checking each room, pausing only when his vision grayed out. His panic mounted when he found her nowhere inside, so he went out through the back door to check out the truck.

Dread sucker-punched him at the sight of the passenger door standing open and the partly shredded upholstery inside. Who the hell had done that? Caitlyn, in a struggle?

A memory sailed back into range, his glimpse of something through the window, something moving inside the truck. Had a vandal done this, or an attacker sick enough to gouge out women's eyes and replace them with cold glass orbs?

"Caitlyn!" Her name rose on a wave of pain, on the dawning certainty that she was nowhere nearby. With the sound of sirens coming nearer, he decided he couldn't trust the police to listen to him. Quickly he gathered his belongings from the house and drove off in the pickup with no idea where to find her, or who might have the stealth, the malice and the skill to coldcock not only him but most likely Reuben Pierce, too, in order to isolate and abduct Caitlyn.

In order to kill her...

Head pounding and face sticky with the clotted blood that had run from his scalp, Marcus risked pulling into a fast food joint with a nearly empty parking lot. Slipping through the side door, he ducked into the restroom and cleaned up enough so he wouldn't be pulled over as he cruised the streets.

Even after the cold-water wash-up, he looked rough, he knew, but he forced himself to take a moment to pick up a large coffee, which he used to wash down a couple of the painkillers he had on him from last night.

Sitting in the parking lot, he pushed aside his lingering pain, his panic and the long-held survival instinct that warned him the police were enemies. Once he reached the NOPD switchboard on his cell phone, he asked to be connected with Detective Robinson, the officer Caitlyn had mentioned in connection with the news about his brother.

"Detective Lorna Robinson," a woman answered.

"This is Marcus Le Carpentier," he started.

"Where are you, Mr. Le Carpentier? We've had officers searching for you all night. Are you all right?"

Not buying into her "concern," Marcus reminded himself to keep the call short, before she could triangulate his location.

"It's for your own safety," Robinson added. "Understand that? You've clearly gotten on the wrong side of the wrong person."

"Tell me about it," he said. "But right now I'm

a lot more worried about Caitlyn Villaré. She's gone missing."

Holding back only the intimate details, he laid out the events of the previous night for the detective, from the gunshots after Caitlyn met him at the cemetery to her disappearance.

"So if you were being hunted, why didn't you call for help last night?" Robinson sounded aggravated. "We know about your brother, what you did for him. And we know from witnesses that the ambulance crash was no accident, that a dark sedan aimed right for it, and that someone shot at you afterwards."

"At the time, I had no idea what you knew or didn't. Or whether I'd end up dead trying to turn myself in. A cop was hurt in that wreck —"

"Killed," Detective Robinson stated flatly.

"I'm sorry to hear it. Really sorry. But considering the circumstances, emotions are bound to be running high. High enough to get a suspect shot."

"You're not a suspect."

"Whatever you say, Detective… But right now, I don't give a damn about what happens to me. All I care about is finding Caitlyn before that bastard decides to…" He couldn't bring himself to name aloud the fears crowding into his mind. "Before he lays a hand on her."

He has already, and you know it. Caitlyn never would have gone without a fight.

"Okay, Marcus. I understand exactly what you're saying," Detective Robinson said. "So do you have any idea where we should be looking? Or who might want to hurt Ms. Villaré?"

He let out a long breath, relieved beyond measure that he'd contacted the one cop who was willing to listen to him. "I'd check up on Josiah Paine, for starters. After I warned him to quit threatening her, the son of a bitch shot me."

"You're saying it was Josiah Paine who shot you?"

"Forget about that right now. I'm only worried about what he might do to Caitlyn."

"He threatened her? Directly?"

"Yesterday. Outside the post office, she said. He implied he had friends who would 'take care of her,' and that he could make the cops look the other way."

"Oh, did he?" Acid edged Robinson's voice. "Let's see that bloated windbag try it on me. I'm certainly not one of his old boy drinking buddies."

"And Paine has an employee, a guy named…" Marcus struggled to dredge up the memory. Something Old Louisiana. Something that reminded him of…*pirates?* "Lafitte, that's it. His name is Max Lafitte, and he hates Caitlyn for showing him up. She said he's got some kind of grudge against her parents, too."

"Her parents?" Lorna Robinson's attention perked up. "They've been dead now for..."

"I'm not sure," Marcus answered, "but she mentioned that her father was murdered."

"Here it is. Back in the eighties," Detective Robinson said. "Not long before those prostitutes were found with the blond wigs and green glass eyes. Was Caitlyn's mama, by any chance, a blonde, too?"

"I have no idea what she looked like. But it's possible, don't you think, that Caitlyn resembles her enough to trigger something like this in a sick mind?"

"One *very* sick mind I'd like to get off the streets and into a cell. So do you have any other ideas for me? Anybody else, while we're out rounding folks up?"

"You might ask Reuben Pierce. Retired cop who works with Caitlyn. He ended up in the hospital with a concussion last night, and I'll lay you odds he was hit by the same guy who knocked me out. I don't know which hospital, though."

"Pierce?" she asked, and in the background, Marcus heard her rapid-fire keystrokes on a computer. "You think he was assaulted? I don't see a report of that here, but maybe it hasn't been logged in yet."

Marcus thought about the dark sedan, so like an officer's unmarked car. He thought about the crash last night, intentionally caused by someone who knew how to hit a vehicle and make it lose control without destroying his own car.

"You know what? Let me check one more thing," Lorna Robinson said. "I ordered Pierce's jacket sent up, but when my partner vouched for him, I didn't make it a priority to... Here, I've got it. Right in the middle of the pile."

Marcus visualized a cubicle with a desk stacked to the ceiling. Homicide in the Big Easy must be one busy department.

"Well, well," said Lorna Robinson, her tone darkening. "You know what, Mr. Le Carpentier? I'm a good cop. Worked damned hard for sixteen years to get myself promoted and transferred here where I am."

Marcus realized then that she was an outsider, a woman who'd fought her way up through the mostly white and mostly male ranks. That might explain her willingness to speak to him so freely. Either that or she was sharp enough to see her candor as the best way of gaining his cooperation.

"I'm tired of corrupt clowns who took the easy way out all their years in, counting on the code of silence to protect them when they tell people they're 'retired.'" She all but spat the word in her disgust. "*Retired* my ass. Reuben Pierce got caught takin' bribes from bad guys about eight years back. Ended up *retirin'* before he could get fired."

"They charged him with corruption?"

"Looks to me like they were just happy to have him gone. Might've been some strings pulled, too, a little of that old boy business, to let him off with his pension. But that's all water under the bridge," she told Marcus. "What I'm wondering right now is, what's this damned dirty cop been up to lately?"

Marcus added grimly, "Does his file mention if any of those bribes he took came from Mr. New Orleans After Dark? I understand the man's running a loan shark business on the side."

"Oh, is he now?" He heard the shuffling of papers before she answered, "I don't see Josiah Paine mentioned in all this, but that doesn't necessarily mean he wasn't involved."

Marcus could easily imagine another of the man's "friends in the department" keeping his name out of it.

"I'm guessing the next thing you'll do," Marcus thought aloud, "is check with other cops and hospitals to find out whether Reuben Pierce was really attacked last night at all."

Chapter Twenty-One

When Caitlyn came to, she heard yelling in the room, a series of shouts that made her cower back onto whatever—a couch? a bed?—he had dumped her on while she was still unconscious.

Pain flared at her slight movement, her neck and throat in agony where he'd choked her from behind during their struggle, and her arm still stinging from whatever had been in the shot he'd used to knock her out. With her sight blurred and head spinning, she made out two figures but could not yet focus on the face of either one.

But though the older woman had her back to Caitlyn, there was something familiar in her voice, something so chilling that it stole the breath from her lungs.

"She can't stay here. I won't have it."

Shock spun through Caitlyn as she realized that this had been last night's caller on her voice mail—the "nurse" who had left the message saying that Reuben was hospitalized with a concussion.

A lie, Caitlyn now realized. Because as she blinked and squinted, Reuben himself came into view. With a cry of disbelief, the full horror of the situation slammed her. Her attacker was the same man she had loved and trusted like a father—a man she and Jacinth had so quickly accepted when he had introduced himself as a family friend and former cop. When he had helped them after their grandmother's funeral. When he had quietly, insidiously, wormed his way into their lives, proving himself so trustworthy and indispensable that Jacinth didn't hesitate to put him on the payroll after Caitlyn started up her business.

"It can't be you," she moaned, willing it to be a nightmare. "You can't— Reuben, it's me. Please, Reuben, please snap out of it!"

"It has to happen here, *Maman*. They're all waiting." Reuben ignored her, looking at the older woman, his voice sounding so little like the man she'd known that Caitlyn had to double-check to be sure she had been right about who he was.

Though his physical features were the same, she saw something hideously unhinged revealed in his eyes.

"Don't you see, Mother?" he asked, his face contorted and terrifying. "The attendants are all ready and the wedding guests assembled. *Our* wedding guests."

Wedding? He means to marry *me?* Horrified, Caitlyn's eyes darted around a musty-smelling room lit only by a glowing lantern in the middle of a filthy floor. She was lying beside it on an aged bed that gave her a view of four walls covered in a peeling floral paper and lined entirely— save for one boarded-over window—in shelf after shelf…

Of dolls of all descriptions…a legion of them. Big dolls, little dolls—there had to be hundreds, casting weirdly elongated shadows whose owners' empty, artificial green eyes stared out from beneath mops of pale blond hair.

She screamed and struggled to get up, only to find that her wrists had been shackled to the wooden bed frame. Crying out as she pulled against the chains, she demanded, "Let me go, you psycho. I'm not about to marry you."

"You hear that, Reuben, boy? You have to get rid of her." His mother's voice cracked, bringing to mind the ancient Eva Rill of the widow's weeds and armed threats.

Though this frail, white-haired woman wore a pastel housedress, Caitlyn realized now that they were one and the same person. *The family that slays together…*

"Eva Rill" reached up, grabbing her son's

collar. "Sophie never wanted you, boy. If she had, she wouldn't have run off and married Villaré. So show some sense, for once in your life, and get rid of the body before they come here looking for you."

The *body?* A rising crop of chill bumps overrode all other horrors. Turning to the saner party, Caitlyn pleaded, "You have to help me, please, ma'am. You have to make him understand that I'm not my mother. Please, for Reuben's sake. I won't tell anyone. I'll work with you to get your son help, if you'll only let me go."

The white-haired woman whipped around with astonishing speed for someone her age, swooping in to hiss in Caitlyn's face, "You little fool—it's all your fault, don't you see? He was so much better after she left town with you and your brat sister. So much better. He had a good job, with good benefits.... He built us a fine house."

If this shabby room were any indication, Caitlyn couldn't say much for the old woman's taste.

"But you had to show up in town, you with your damned hair and those cat's eyes. Shaking your tail feathers in his face just like your—"

Caitlyn shook her head emphatically. "No. It wasn't like that. Reuben was— He's always been a friend, almost like an uncle to me. That's all. I swear I never—"

"I did *everything* I could to convince you to

leave. I went along with his fool plan, got you to the cemetery so you could see what you'd made him do again, for the first time in such a long time. I even showed up at your house, waved that gun in your face and shot through your window. Yet you still refused to run."

"I didn't understand. I swear it."

The sound of a crack filled the room before she even registered the old woman's bony slap.

Cheek stinging, she listened as Reuben's mother insisted, "Your slut mama ruined his life. Did she ever tell you? She promised she would marry him. Later on, she tried to laugh it off, pretend it was nothing but a misunderstanding, a flirtation. Claimed she was joking, that's all. Because all the while she was leading my poor boy around by his pecker, she was carrying on with a man from an old family, a man with money, not some dirty whore's son from the wrong side of the—"

"Don't say that, *Maman.* Please don't say it," Reuben whimpered. "It's about to be all better. I know how to fix it this time."

"I'm not Sophie Sinclair!" Caitlyn screamed, tears burning her face. "She was my mother, and she died."

As if he hadn't heard her, the man she'd once thought she knew kept speaking. "And I know I have to punish her, the same as all the rest."

Tipped off by the detective in return for his co-operation after Caitlyn's rescue, Marcus watched from a safe distance as at least a dozen officers, including a SWAT team decked out all in black, formed a cautious circle surrounding a modest but neat one-story blue house in the Garden District.

Clearly they were taking Reuben seriously as a suspect, after confirming that he was in none of the area hospitals and hadn't filed a police report the previous night. From the looks of the heavy gear, they were anticipating trouble, too—the armed mayhem that a serial murderer, familiar with guns from his work, might choose to dish out if he felt cornered.

Behind a dark van, a heavyset black woman in a brown skirt stood with a phone pressed to her ear and her arms ringed with six or eight multicolor bracelets. After a minute she put away the phone and returned from the dark van with a bullhorn, which she raised to her lips.

"This is Detective Lorna Robinson, NOPD. I need the occupants of 1407 South Mockingbird to exit the house with your hands on top of your head. Either that, or answer your phone. We'll give you one more chance to do that so we can clear up a few questions."

She pointed to a balding white man, who raised

a phone to his ear. After several long moments he shook his head and put the phone away.

Detective Robinson repeated her request. When no one emerged, she gave a nod to two armored men from the SWAT team.

Trampling flower beds, they hurried toward the front door carrying a long black cylinder. Two-man battering ram, Marcus decided, which meant that Robinson had either come up with one fast warrant or decided that imminent danger trumped the need for one.

With two quick pops, the door burst inward, and the officers unslung their automatic weapons and raced inside. Wishing he could be there, that he could be the one to strafe the traitor with a hail of bullets and carry Caitlyn to safety, Marcus waited with his breath held and prayed with all his might.

He strained his ears, hungering for, and at the same time dreading, the sound of gunfire or a shrill cry. But a scream would at least mean someone inside was still living—as long as it wasn't Caitlyn's death cry, if Reuben decided he wasn't going to give her up alive.

Instead of shouts or shots, there was nothing but silence. A silence that finally ended in an indistinct squawk from someone's radio.

Soon all the officers moved inside, while behind the screen of shrubbery that hid him,

Marcus's heart continued pounding. Had they made an arrest? Learned Caitlyn was safe or badly injured?

Or had they found her lifeless body hidden in the house?

WHEN A PHONE RANG IN ANOTHER ROOM, Reuben strode toward Caitlyn as his mother went to answer.

Caitlyn thought of trying to gain the caller's help by screaming. Instead, seeing the madness in her former employee's eye, she shrank back, every muscle quivering with the instinctive need to bolt.

This was the man who had already killed at least six women. Who, for all she knew, had murdered Marcus in order to catch her on her own.

Grief rolled over her, wave after wave that brought tears to her eyes and had her hissing through her clenched teeth, "You stay away from me, you bastard."

"You shut up." Reuben sprang onto the bed, onto *her,* and though she pummeled him with her knees and her chained hands, she was helpless to stop him from pinning her down and shoving his face to within an inch of hers.

Her silent tears flowed freely as he leaned low and whispered near her ear, "Listen, Sophie, we have to keep real quiet while *Maman*'s on the phone."

Too frightened to either argue or contradict his use of her mother's name, Caitlyn could do nothing but listen to the harsh rasp of Reuben's breath and the murmur of the old woman's conversation—a conversation that sounded impossibly casual, as if her son were not about to...

Caitlyn refused to let her mind go further. Refused to despair, to give up on the chance of getting out of here alive. Getting out and back to Marcus, where—if he'd somehow survived—she would beg him to forgive her for pushing away the slightest chance that they might someday be together.

She had to help him straighten everything out back in Pennsylvania, to convince him to stay with her—or at the very least make him understand that she hadn't shared her body lightly. That she loved him deeply and wanted far more than just one night.

Reuben shifted his bulk to lie on top of her as he spoke roughly into her ear. "You're mine now, Sophie. I'm finally going to have you, after all these years."

Struggling against his weight, against the terrifying hardness she felt jutting into her thigh, Caitlyn bit down on his shoulder. Shouting with pain, Reuben leapt off her, balling his huge fist and drawing it back.

Though tethered by her shackles, Caitlyn still managed to dodge the blow. Cursing her roundly, he looked primed for murder—until his mother came back into the room, a cell phone in her hand and disgust in her eyes.

"I'm sorry, *Maman*," he said. "Sorry for the swears."

The glass-eyed audience and tattered walls spun around Caitlyn. He'd been about to assault and possibly kill her, and now he was apologizing to his mother for cursing?

If she somehow survived this family's insanity, she swore she would give her beautiful, brilliant and caring sister the biggest hug of her life.

"That was our neighbor, Mrs. DeHart. They're breaking into our house, Reuben!" Set amid so many wrinkles, the old woman's eyes were wide with outrage—or maybe it was terror. "*Our house!* The police, with SWAT teams. So just how long do you imagine it will be before they track you here and shoot you down like a mad dog?"

Caitlyn's hope flared, only to be crushed when Reuben spoke.

"They'll never find this place. It's not even in my name."

"They'll find you, son. They'll kill you. You have to take care of this problem and dump the body somewhere *now*."

Chapter Twenty-Two

Nothing. They'd found nothing. Marcus felt ready to burst out of his skin by the time he finally understood that the slowdown in activity and dispersal of the SWAT team meant that no one had been inside, neither the living or the dead.

Rather than being reassured, Marcus felt even more helpless with the realization that Reuben had some other kill zone, separate from his home. Elsewhere…but where? He thought of past news stories, detailing serial murderers who dug out hidden trap-door basements beneath their houses or disguised backyard dungeons as tool sheds, but he didn't think that the NOPD—especially Detective Lorna Robinson—was stupid enough to skip a thorough search and miss such a hideout. Just as certainly, the police were likely to check property tax rolls to find out if their suspect owned a second place, perhaps even an isolated fishing cabin on the bayou.

The thought of Caitlyn trapped and surrounded

by nothing but a maze of gator-infested water-ways had Marcus shaking with the need to find Reuben and kill him with his bare hands. But anger wouldn't help him, so he thrust it roughly out of his way and tried to focus on the most important question he would ever have to answer in his life.

Where else might a killer take his quarry? Where would he feel safe, secure, familiar, in effortless control?

There's no place like home.... No place like home... The familiar refrain repeated in Marcus's mind, echoing over and over until his head pounded with its rhythm and the words jumbled into gibberish.

It reminded him that he had what was undoubtedly a concussion, on top of the bullet wound. He shouldn't even be on his feet, much less shaking off his pain to weave back toward his parked truck.

And the last thing he had any business doing was climbing back behind the wheel.

But the noise inside his head had given him a flash of insight, the long-shot sliver of an idea of the one other place where Reuben might have taken Caitlyn. As crazy as it seemed, once the thought formed, he couldn't shake it.

Leaving the police to whatever leads they might find in either Reuben's home or Caitlyn's,

Marcus cranked the engine and drove off to follow up his wild hunch.

A hunch that would take him to one of the most crime-ridden areas of New Orleans—if his wavering vision and the worsening pounding in his head didn't cause him to wreck the truck on the way.

"WE CAN'T LEAVE, *Maman*. I won't do it. Don't you see, the priest is here now. He's come to marry us." Rather than shouting as he had been, Reuben had gone dead calm, speaking in a tone so chillingly reasonable that Caitlyn half expected to see a man in black materialize, a clerical collar on his neck.

"Now, Reuben," said his mother. "I won't tell you again."

Her son smiled back at her. "This is the happiest day of my life."

Turning with a huff of disgust, the old woman left the room and slammed the door behind her.

A shudder traveling through her, Caitlyn yanked against her bonds as hard as she could and was rewarded by the crack of the wood at her left side splitting. Splitting, but not breaking through completely.

Reuben turned and frowned down at her. "In a hurry, are we?" With his wink, the sickening smile returned. "Tell you a little secret. So am I."

Pulling a key from his shirt pocket, he said, "Here. Let me help you up, so you can stand before God and our guests."

Caitlyn froze as he approached her, wondering how she could reach the sane, protective man she had known for months. The madness in his eyes convinced her that man was out of reach—probably forever—so she decided to try to use his insanity to her advantage. She racked her brain to think of some way—something she might do or say—to get free before Reuben moved on from the marriage to the "honeymoon," a thought that filled her with more terror than the specter of her murder.

Calling on her theater training, she steeled herself to play the hardest role of her life—before the toughest crowd.

"I'm a little embarrassed," she whispered to the maniac who had cast himself as her groom as he moved to free her. "It's our wedding day, and I haven't even had the chance to freshen up. My hair, my makeup— I'll look just awful for our pictures."

"You're beautiful, Sophie. Every bit as lovely as you always have been."

She flashed him a coquettish smile, despite her churning stomach. "But a girl likes to look *special* on her special day, and besides, I really need to powder my nose."

Please let him be as crazy as he looks this minute, she prayed. *And please, God, whatever you do, let the bathroom in this dive have a window.*

He studied her, a measuring look, while she held her breath, waiting for his answer. Waiting to find out if, in his delusional state, she might have fooled him, or whether her last-ditch gamble had failed.

She would never know the answer, because at that moment the bedroom door burst open and Reuben's mother came in gripping a pistol in both hands, which trembled with the weight of the big long-barreled weapon.

"It's time," she said to Reuben as Caitlyn edged behind her captor. "Time I took care of this so I can get you somewhere safe."

"No, *Maman.* You can't." His voice became a low growl. "I told you before, I'm *going* to kill her. I'm not stupid. But I'm going to do it on my own terms and in my own time."

His glare swung to Caitlyn, and he grabbed her by the arm with bruising pressure.

"*After* we've played out our little wedding game," he said quietly. "Played it by *my* rules."

"No. No, Reuben." The old woman sounded resigned, broken—until she swung the gun toward Caitlyn's chest and her finger moved on the trigger.

Chapter Twenty-Three

Everything had limits. Endurance, will—and even soul-deep love, Marcus discovered, as the backwash of adrenaline slammed him with a vengeance.

One moment he was jamming the key into his ignition, and the next he was lying slumped sideways, his vision narrowed to a pinhole tunnel through black wool.

Fighting off unconsciousness, he embraced the pain exploding in his right arm and ricocheting inside his skull in the hope that it would rouse him. Yet the black tunnel only tightened, constricting slowly until he saw nothing, felt nothing, knew nothing but a swiftly fading sense of loss.

Sometime later, he felt vibration. Next the ringing of a telephone burrowed its way into his awareness.

Groping for it, he opened his eyes and recognized the truck's dashboard, though everything was out of focus. He ignored the phone and managed to get the truck started as panic jolted through him. How the hell long had he been out? Had he missed his chance to get to Caitlyn before it was too late?

Head still swimming, he started driving and blew through a stop sign, then slammed on the brakes and fishtailed, his truck careening narrowly around a brightly painted daycare van. Cursing, he checked the rearview to see that the woman driving looked shaken but okay and her vehicle remained in control.

"Pull yourself together," he told himself. The last thing he wanted was to kill someone before he got there.

Once he arrived—and assuming his hunch was right—it would be another story. Because if putting down the rabid pit bull was what it took to save the woman he loved, this time he would do it.

Would do what he should have done for Samantha. What he wished, God help him, he had done to Theo before his only brother went on to kill again.

AGE MIGHT HAVE ITS PRIVILEGES, but hand strength seemed not to be among them. As Reuben's mother struggled to pull the trigger, her son lunged to grab the gun.

Too scared to scream, Caitlyn didn't waste

an instant, ducking under his arm and racing through the doorway. Once past it, she flew down a narrow hallway with holes in its moldy Sheetrock walls and torn wads of carpet that sent up a sour stink with every step.

As fast as she was moving, one of those clumps tripped her, sending her crashing to her hands and knees as shots cracked above her head and bullets popped against a boarded-up window.

"Hold it right there, Caitlyn," Reuben ordered. "Stop now, or I swear I'll shoot you."

Caitlyn didn't move a muscle, her vision drifting to the left and locking onto what appeared to be the once-white front door of the small house, her sole escape route from this hell.

A dirty yellow waterline sliced across it halfway up, confirming her suspicion that this place was a flood house, one of those still awaiting demolition post-Katrina. But the detail that brought tears to her eyes was the cool gleam of the mint-condition latch and heavy-duty padlock someone had put on that door. And she would bet her legacy, her very future, that the only key was in the bottom of Reuben Pierce's pocket.

She was never getting out of here, at least not alive.

Still, her desperate mind groped for an escape, for the slightest detail that might help her talk Reuben out of—

Slowly she turned to look over her shoulder. Reuben was standing there, his jaw tight and the barrel of his pistol steady as it pointed straight at her chest.

"Ready to join me at the altar?" he asked as calmly as if he were offering her a cup of coffee.

Thinking of slaughtered lambs and sacrificial altars, she shook her head and said, "You called me Caitlyn. I heard you. So you know I'm not Sophie."

Pure malice lighting his gaze, he stalked his way toward her and grabbed her by the hair. "It's your eyes, you see. They aren't quite the same green, are they?"

From the doll room came the sound of sobbing, Reuben's mother weeping as though her heart were broken.

Caitlyn felt her own heart freeze, followed by an awareness of it pumping icy terror through every vein and artery, every capillary, in her body.

"But don't worry, my sweet Caitlyn. I have the perfect pair here for you. They're *exactly* the right shade."

MARCUS DROVE SLOWLY along Noble Street in Midtown, his attention straining as he took in the mix of vacant lots and dilapidated bungalows. The nearby housing projects had been torn down, but this low area, with its longstanding bad reputation, hadn't been rebuilt, and a good number of boarded-up, flood-ravaged houses stood forgotten in spite of the red X's spray painted on their doors.

Though his dash clock didn't work, the sun's position told him it was getting close to noon, as did the heat waves rising from the broken asphalt.

There was not a soul in sight, leading him to believe any current residents had chosen to sleep away the daylight hours.

Praying for some sign to confirm his hunch about Reuben, he checked out empty front stoops and a couple of mangy, spotted dogs sniffing halfheartedly at the contents of a split black trash bag.

This was crazy, hopeless, he realized, as he scanned the few cars, some of them stripped and burned out, parked along the street or in what had once been front yards.

Even on the remote chance she might be somewhere near, he would never find her. Would fail her just as he had failed…

That was when it caught his eye. A shape unlike the others. Slowing to a crawl, he spotted something alongside a tiny, peeling shack with a half-collapsed front porch. A gray shroud covered what could only be a parked car.

A car that looked to be the size and shape of Reuben Pierce's dark sedan.

Several houses down, Marcus pulled over to the broken curb and bailed out, cell phone in hand. Halfway through dialing Detective Robinson, he stopped himself, wondering if the whack to his head had blown out one of his fuses. Surely she would think him insane if he bothered her without a single shred of evidence.

Half hope, half prayer, his conviction that she was here grew as he rushed toward the gray shroud, keeping his head low to lessen the chance he might be spotted through a crack between the boards covering the windows.

Reaching the vehicle, he grabbed the cover and began lifting—an instant before shots echoed loudly from inside the house.

Chapter Twenty-Four

In the split second it took Reuben to release her hair and grab for her arm, Caitlyn kicked out with the force of desperation. Whether by blind luck or instinct, she caught the back of Reuben's knees. As his legs collapsed, he went down with a shout of rage.

Springing to her feet, she raced down the short hall, turning to the right, away from the locked door, just as Reuben started blasting away, cursing her with every shot.

She wildly searched the dark space for even the tiniest fleck of sunlight, anything that might suggest a blocked window she might break through to escape. Before she found what she was looking for, the shooting came to an abrupt halt.

She tried but couldn't think back to count how many shots he'd fired—or how many bullets the pistol might hold. Could the gun have jammed? And if it had, would he have a backup weapon, maybe a second gun strapped to his ankle?

Straining her ears for the slightest sign of movement, she heard only the old woman's keening, "My hip, my hip. Please come help me, Reuben."

Do it. Play the good son. So what if she's as insane as you are?

As Caitlyn felt her way around what might have served as kitchen counters, she heard the soft clunk of a door closing, cutting off the dim illumination cast by the lantern in the doll room. Had Reuben closed himself inside with his injured mother, or shut the door against her cries in order to stalk Caitlyn in the darkness?

She shuddered, biting back a scream at the thought of him grabbing her at any moment, a deadly game of blind man's bluff. *If* he was in here somewhere with her instead of seeing to his mother…

Her head jerked to the right. Had she heard the scrape of a rough breath? The echo of a footstep? Rushing in the opposite direction, she cried out as she knocked the point of her hip against something hard and unyielding. A porcelain sink? A stove?

She heard his gloating laughter closing in on her, an obscene parody of all the easy chuckles they had shared these past few months. As she bolted out of reach, she heard a voice, muffled but unmistakable, from the other side of the wall.

"Caitlyn? Are you in there? I can't get in! The doors are all locked!"

"Marcus!" she cried, scarcely believing he had found her. That he was still alive. "Marcus, it's Reuben! Call the police. He has a—"

A gun, she'd meant to say, before bullets drilled the air around her and the burnt-powder scent filled her nose. Once more she lurched away, not knowing or much caring whether she'd been hit or not, only that her legs worked.

"Where the hell are you, bitch?" Reuben shouted. "Tell me now and I won't shoot."

As she groped her way to the other side of the room, Caitlyn encountered something wooden and upright. A loose board? No. It felt more like furniture. Realizing that the table was upside down and she'd encountered one of its legs, she planted one foot on the underside of its top and yanked at the loose piece until it came away with a satisfying crack....

A crack that informed Reuben exactly where she was.

Still shouting at the 9-1-1 dispatcher, Marcus raced back to the truck and tossed his cell phone onto the seat beside him without even bothering to disconnect. He cranked the engine and jammed it into gear, his panic mounting with the knowledge that every second wasted might be Caitlyn's last.

He couldn't allow himself to think she might be dead already. That any of the shots he'd heard could have pierced some vital organ. Instead he jammed his foot to the floor and lurched forward, the truck's front right corner catching and tearing off the bumper of the abandoned car ahead of it, flinging the metal in its wake. Slewing to the right, the pickup jumped the curb and roared toward the padlocked shack.

The four-wheel-drive jounced forward, gaining speed with every foot it chewed up. Both hands clenching the steering wheel, he aimed toward the side of the house farthest from the spot Caitlyn's voice had come from. A moment before impact, he braced himself and flung a desperate prayer to heaven that he wouldn't end up doing more harm than good.

With an enormous crash, the pickup tore into the little house, the airbag exploding into Marcus's face before the truck jerked to a stop. He recovered within seconds, then threw open the door to see only clouds of dust swirling like smoke all around him, to hear only the creak and clatter of settling roof timbers, and the drip of water somewhere.

Scarcely daring to breathe, he peered into the settling dust and spotted a host of arms and legs, bent at impossible angles and torn from lifeless torsos, some of them crumpled on the truck's hood. And glittering green glass eyes, all wide with accusation. Wide and utterly empty.

What the hell? *Dolls?*

Flaxen-haired dolls of every size and type he could imagine lay scattered everywhere. Yet something drew his gaze to the twisted arm of one of the largest, jutting from beneath a slab of collapsed roofing a few feet in front of where his truck had come to rest.

Oh, God, no. He saw the blood now. A pool spreading from one mostly buried body. He ran to lift the limp wrist, too slender to be Reuben's. Had his actions taken Caitlyn's life?

Beneath his searching fingers, no pulse fluttered. But he quickly realized that this arm—this wrinkled, bony, lifeless limb—was far too thin and frail to be—

"Marcus!" Caitlyn shrieked behind him. "Help me. Please make him—let *go,* you sick, demented—"

With every word, he heard the heavy *thunk* of something hard impacting flesh. Lurching toward the sound, Marcus peered through the choking dust, and spotted Caitlyn beating Pierce's back and shoulder with a squared-off length of wood while he clung desperately to her ankle with one hand.

The other, Marcus saw, was reaching for a gun. Clambering through a snow of insulation and over fallen two-by-fours, Marcus reached the prone man and grabbed him by the back of his neck. Despite Reuben's greater weight and Marcus's own injuries, he yanked Pierce back, rolling him over and slamming his fist into the ex-cop's face.

As the impact of the blow crunched bone, an arc of blood flew from the killer's smashed nose. Barely feeling the agony radiating up his arm, Marcus pounded him again and again until the man fell completely limp.

"Is he...?" Caitlyn managed to ask.

"Out cold, thank God." As hard as Marcus had hit him, he wasn't sure Reuben would ever wake again. Not that he gave a damn about that.

Kicking away the gun, Marcus turned to haul a dirty, bruised and weeping Caitlyn into his arms. "Are you hurt? Did he shoot you or...?"

"I—I'm all right, I think, or at least I will be once I...Marcus, are you really here, or did I dream you?" Shudders racked her body, yet her breath was warm in his ear. Warm. Alive. And to Marcus, that was everything that mattered. His limbs were shaking with relief.

"You're awake, Caitlyn. Awake and safe, and the police are on their way."

She clutched at him. "Please don't run again. Please don't leave me here alone with them."

The terror in her voice made his gut clench,

filling him with regret for the times he had been forced to flee when she needed him.

"I'll stay until I'm sure you're safe." He squeezed her tighter, then softly kissed the slightly damp hair at her temple. "And someday, Caitlyn, if I'm able and you'll have me..."

She pulled back to look into his eyes. "If I'll *have* you? What do you mean, Marcus?"

"I know I have no right, but I'm saying that I love you, and I want to be with you. Forever."

Her beautiful green eyes flared, and his heart sank. He realized how unwelcome his offer must be, when he had so little to offer. With almost nothing to his name but risk, he had been right from the beginning. He couldn't drag her into his cursed life.

"I'm sorry," he said, each word costing a chunk of his soul. "I can't do this to you. Because you deserve the white horse and the carriage. The fancy dinners and the roses. The Bourbon Street dates and the jazz bands and every single thing you've ever wanted, leading up to a proposal on bended knee. And you deserve all of it from a man who's able to give you the kind of future that will make you happy."

"You think I want *dates,* Marcus?" she asked. "You think I'm standing here this minute expecting a bouquet, a tuxedo and a ring? Or a crystal ball to guarantee a perfect future?"

"You *should* want all those things. God knows, I want them for you."

Sirens wailed like lost souls in the distance, so many that he wondered if the whole police force was closing in on their location.

Blinking away tears, Caitlyn draped her arms around his neck and leaned close so he would hear her. "I know exactly what I want. A man who's loyal, who's proven that he values family—even family members who have hurt him deeply. A man who's braver and stronger than anyone I've ever known before, who makes me feel things no one else ever has. A man just like you, Marcus, who's saved my life and absolutely won my heart."

She turned to meet his lips, and within that damaged, crumbling house of evil, something pure and perfect pierced his grief.

When at last their lingering mouths parted, she smiled up to tell him, "I would love to be with you, only you, forever."

Epilogue

Three weeks later...

In an old French Quarter cemetery that cradled saints and sinners alike, twilight stained the western sky bloodred. As she led her tour group through the gates, Caitlyn's imagination cut a swath through the ghost of a lost morning's fog, which sent soft eddies of memory swirling all around her.

Heart pounding, her gaze darted forward, traveling toward the gravesite where a false ruby flanked with "diamonds" had once winked in the dawn's light.

Toward the place where she had discovered a stone-dead body and a soul-deep love....

"Miss Villaré?" a soft voice prompted, causing her to blink and nod to Jimmy, the strapping young intern she had taken on to help with the business.

She began to talk, regaling her audience with

tales of the old Vieux Carré, as many locals called the Quarter. Soon she was responding to eager questions and pointing out the differences between the different types of tombs. But the longer she explained the various funerary symbols on them—the lambs and weeping willows, the anchors and the open book—the more her gaze kept straying to the ethereal angel Marcus had photographed with such skill, hoping to conjure the man himself back from his trip to square everything with Pennsylvania authorities and risk a face-to-face discussion with Samantha's vengeful father. She'd been scared to death, barely able to sleep or eat, until Marcus called to reassure her that the former criminal was a changed man, a man who had renounced his violent past and finally accepted that nothing could ever bring back his daughter.

Feeling a presence behind her, Caitlyn glanced over her shoulder, then gasped at the silhouette of a tall and well-formed figure, a man she knew even before his face emerged from shadow.

"Marcus, you're back!" She raced to throw herself into strong arms she'd longed to feel again.

As Jimmy deftly led the tour group out of earshot, Marcus hugged her to his chest and kissed her temple.

"I've missed you so much. I was all set to fly

back, and then I received word that my mentor, Isaiah Jericho, was dying."

"Isaiah Jericho?" she asked, recognizing the famed photographer's name.

Marcus nodded. "He was asking for me, fading fast, so I raced to the airport and grabbed the first flight I could."

"Did you make it?" she asked gently.

"Just in time," he said, the line of his mouth somber. "Thank God. And then I got the next flight to New Orleans, and here I am." He pulled her closer, then said, "And I have some good news, too.

"Isaiah left me some money. Quite a lot, actually. And before he died, he released a statement confessing to collaborating with me as he passed on his techniques. I was expecting the worst when he admitted misleading buyers, but I've been amazed at the outpouring of support. He left a trust to compensate any collectors who felt deceived, but so far, there haven't been any takers."

He sounded both awed and grateful. "My new agent says I have a great shot at making a living with my photography."

Heedless of the dead around them, he dropped to one knee before her. "And now that I have something real to offer the woman I'm in love with…"

Noticing that her group of tourists—along with her new intern—had turned to smile her way, Caitlyn whispered furiously, "Get up, Marcus. Please. Everyone is watching."

"I don't give a damn," he told her. "I only care about making you believe that from this point on, wherever you are is my home. You're my life and my future, as long as you'll have me."

When she looked into his dark eyes, she saw the passion in them, the intensity of a bond that would carry them through the years together...

And through the birth of the child she would tell him later that they were expecting. But for now, she couldn't speak, couldn't do anything but tug him back onto his feet and kiss him.

The first kiss of a forever she could not wait to begin.

* * * * *

LARGER-PRINT BOOKS!
GET 2 FREE LARGER-PRINT NOVELS PLUS
2 FREE GIFTS!

◆ **Harlequin**

INTRIGUE

BREATHTAKING ROMANTIC SUSPENSE

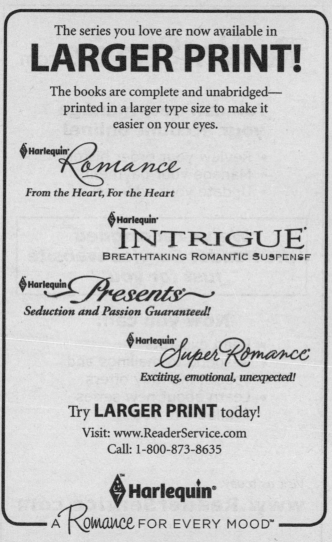